The Red Trail

Bucko Martin was a bronco-buster who thought he'd get an easier job with the Union Pacific Railroad, but he was in for a traumatic surprise. A U.P. train was ambushed by a bunch of renegade Indians and the soldiers on board massacred. Then Bucko's brother was killed and he swore to hunt down the culprits.

Into his world came two famed characters known throughout the territory. First there was Buffalo Bill and then the famous Wild Bill Hickock. All were bound together to apprehend the murdering Indians and the palefaces who were supplying them with rifles.

This dramatic novel of non-stop action is a brilliant re-creation of life in the brutal, unforgiving days of the Old West.

The Red Trail

BRAD SHANNON

A Black Horse Western

ROBERT HALE · LONDON

© 1951, 2003 Vic J. Hanson.
First hardcover edition 2003
Originally published in paperback as
The Red Trail by V. Joseph Hanson

ISBN 0 7090 7260 0

Robert Hale Limited
Clerkenwell House
Clerkenwell Green
London EC1R 0HT

Typeset by
Derek Doyle & Associates, Liverpool.
Printed and bound in Great Britain by
Antony Rowe Limited, Wiltshire.

ONE

The driver of the train yelled frenziedly and pulled hard at the brake. The engineer, who was feeding logs into the firebox half turned. Then, his hands wrapped round his face, he leapt. He hit the ground in a ball, rolling. He stopped, rose to his haunches, sick and dazed as he watched a tragedy he was powerless to avert.

The engine hit the pile of logs which had been placed on the track just around the bend. Then it rose high in the air like a living creature trying to leap over the obstacle. The carriages piled up behind it, steel and wood crumpling and tearing like paper. The din was hideous but over and above it all rose the piercing shrieks of agonized human voices.

The driver had been thrown from the engine and lay squirming like a wingless fly. 'Bob,' croaked the engineer. He rose to his feet, tottering... The poised engine suddenly burst into flame and rolled over. The squirming man on the ground screamed once and then was engulfed in fire and smoke and tumbling wreckage.

The fire travelled to the carriages. All weakness left the engineer and he began to run towards the sound of the imploring voices. At the back of the train soldiers were leaping and tumbling from the carriages. Some of them were overturned or lying beside the line. The free men began to hack with rifle-butts and bayonets, even to tear with their bare hands to let their comrades out.

The fire was travelling fast. The engineer was beaten away by the flames. He could do nothing up there. He tried to shut his ears to the piercing shrieks of those who were being roasted alive. He ran to help the soldiers. With startling suddenness he stopped in his tracks, his hands clawing the air. A brightly-feathered arrow transfixed him. It had gone right through his body: the bloodstained barb protruded from his chest. He tried to scream, to yell a warning, but the sounds only bubbled in his throat. His eyes glazed over. He fell forward on his face.

But one of the blue-clad troopers had seen the incident. 'Injuns!' he bawled. 'Look out – Injuns!' Then he looked around him frantically. His rifle was inside the wrecked train. He had lost his revolver as he tumbled free. Like many of his companions he had no weapon.

A lean young captain who was bending over a wounded man grabbed the revolver beside him and turned. The arrows came thick and fast. A trooper cursed and grabbed at one in his leg. 'Firing positions,' yelled the young officer.

As the Indians came pouring over the rise those soldiers who had weapons formed themselves into two lines, one behind the other. Those in front dropped on one knee, the others stood erect. The men who had pistols only stationed themselves in the front line, the young officer among them. The rest of the men searched frenziedly in the wreckage behind for firearms. All the time the fire travelled steadily along the length of the train but the shrieks of the trapped people were drowned by the blood-chilling war cries of the savages as they charged.

'Cheyennes an' Crows an' a few Sioux.' said one hard-bitten trooper. 'An' by God, look! Pawnees. Renegades!'

'Them ain't Pawnees,' spat another older man. 'You'll never see a Pawnee ridin' with a Sioux. They're jest wearin' old slit cavalry britches they took from some pore devils like us.'

'Not so much o' the pore devils,' snapped the young man. 'Look, I tell yuh. Renegades! White men!'

'By God, yes! About half-a-dozen of 'em. Shore is a passel all told. Must be . . .

The young officer's ringing command drowned the rest of his speech and still talking and cursing to himself the old trooper squeezed the trigger. The firing was steady along the back line in which he stood. Ejected shells from the Winchester repeaters spun and glittered in the air. The front ranks of Indians were swept down as if by a huge scythe. So packed together were they that even the most unlicked conscript could not miss.

But the savages behind came on like shrieking demons, riding over tumbled men and horses. The old trooper noted that the white men had drawn back now, leaving the leadership to a handful of feathered chiefs. The trooper whooped shrilly as he brought one headdress-adorned warrior tumbling from his mount. Then he swung his rifle and drew a bead on a white man, a big dark brute, who in common with the others of his ilk, had a bandanna tied across the lower half of his face. The trooper squeezed the trigger and gave another wild whoop as the big man swayed in the saddle and pitched to the ground.

'That's one o' the dirty renegades!'

He turned at a bubbling scream in his ear. His younger neighbour was crumpling, tearing at the arrow that protruded from his stomach like some fantastic feathered growth. He writhed as his comrade bent over him. Then he lay suddenly still.

He was still alive however. The oldster knew it might be fatal to try to remove the shaft. He dragged the unconscious man behind the line. He saw two dead ones as he did so.

The back line men were reloading their rifles. The Redskins were nearer but in confusion as the pistolees opened up. Their horses were shot from under them, they ran forward wielding tomahawks. But very few of them got to grips. A big trooper wrestled with a hideously painted brave, threw him, and blew his brains out as he tried to rise. Another trooper's skull was cleaved in half by a mighty blow of a shining tomahawk. His slayer was shot immediately.

Many over-zealous young braves threw their lives away against this stolid line. Then the chiefs and sub-chiefs began to turn and retreat and they followed. Riflemen picked them off until, as they began to disappear over the rise, the young captain called 'Cease fire!'

But the fire crackled on, this time from the other side, and all around soldiers began to fall.

'By God, they got guns,' said an old trooper. 'Them damn renegades!'

'Take cover!' shouted the officer.

Dragging their wounded with them they sought the meagre cover of the now smoking wreckage of the train.

To the practised ears of the soldiers it was evident that there were many more than half-a-dozen rifles. Either there were more white men up there who had not shown themselves or some of the Indians had firearms.

One trooper surveyed the brown sprawling figures of dead savages in front of him and said: 'They ought to've picked us off in the fust place. It'd saved 'em a lot o' grief.'

'That ain't the Injun way,' said another. 'They like to come in an' get ye. This is probably the idea o' them damn renegades.'

'Hold your fire,' yelled the young captain. 'Make sure of your cover.'

'Trouble is there ain't any,' said a man. Those were the last words he spoke. A heavy slug bloodily obliterated his face. A hardened trooper near him shuddered involuntarily. 'Somebody up there has a Sharps,' he said.

From behind their pitiful cover the soldiers held their fire and watched. They could see very little to shoot at anyway. Meanwhile many of them were picked off like sitting-ducks.

But the captain, young as he was, knew his Indians. The rifle fire abated and they came over the rise in a screaming mass.

'This is it!' yelled a trooper half in panic as the horde swept nearer. They were an awesome and terrifying sight and their weird cries were enough to chill the heart of the bravest.

An old trooper moved his quid of tobacco from one cheek to the other and spat in black embers beneath his chin. 'Seems more than ever,' he said. 'Ah, wal – it's been a good life.'

'Yes,' said his neighbour, then suddenly rose to his feet, screaming, an arrow in his neck. Then he stopped screaming suddenly and fell like a log, three more arrows in him. The Sioux snipers up on the ridge weren't going to miss a target like that.

The other man cursed. 'Fire!' bawled the officer.

Men fired till the stocks of their rifles were red-hot; loaded and reloaded. The terrible realization began to dawn on all of them as they fumbled at bandoliers. There was very little ammunition left! And the savages came on, washing over their own dead like water over rocks.

'Fixed bayonets,' yelled the officer.

His order to charge never came for he collapsed with an arrow in his breast.

But the remains of the little troop did not need orders now. They rose and fought frenziedly, driving bayonets to the hilt in stinking, paint-bedaubed red bodies, wrestling with dismounted savages, using pistols and rifles as clubs.

Indians were all around them now; there was no sign of the white renegades. They had left their red brothers to finish the job.

The four horsemen saw the smoke from afar.

'Camp-fire,' said the lean redheaded one.

'Camp-fire nuthin',' said the tubby one scornfully. 'That's somethin' big smoulderin' – buildin's, or somethin'.'

The other two were dark and blocky. They looked like brothers. They did not speak.

All four were dressed pretty much alike, in wide-brimmed Stetsons, faded check flannel-shirts, bandannas around their throats, greasy chaps on their bowed horsemen's legs. They all wore low slung guns. Their slickers and bedrolls were strapped behind them.

They urged their horses into a jog-trot, changing their direction a little to make for the bluish drifting smoke-haze.

Ten minutes riding brought them to the rising ground. They climbed and breasted it, then, with characteristic exclamations, reined in their horses and looked down at the smouldering wreckage of the train and the still forms dotted around it like crumpled, broken dolls.

The only living things in sight were the turkey-buzzards, hovering ever nearer and crying plaintively for food.

One of the dark young men spoke now. 'Come on,' he said, and urged his horse down the slope. The others followed. Their horses were restive at the sickly smell of blood and the bright red patches on the ground past which they had to be almost forced.

'Indians,' said the dark young man.

'I don't see no Indians,' said his brother.

'They allus take their dead with 'em . . . But come and look at their handiwork.'

He dismounted and stood gentling his horse with his hands. At his feet were two bodies. The others dismounted and joined him. The tubby one took one look then turned away and began to retch.

Both bodies were naked. A cavalry-man's hat beside the one was the only clue to their identity. They had both been scalped. But that wasn't all. Their noses had been slit, their eyes poked out, their ears sliced. And their bodies had been cut into fantastic, horrible patterns.

'The red devils suttinly made a job of these two,' said the first dark young man. 'I tol' you boys this wasn't a nice country.'

But his comrades had turned away, had moved over to step among other bodies lain closer together as if in sleep, all along the smoke-blackened railroad lines and amid the crumbling rubble. Every single one had been scalped but the savages hadn't bothered to strip completely any more of them. Probably they had tried to outdo each other in taking of the gory trophies which every brave treasured.

Scared by the intruders the buzzards had retreated and flapped in the distance. Their cries came faintly on the still air.

'Lets get out of here,' called the tubby man.

'Yeh,' said the quieter of the two brothers. 'We cain't do nuthin' here. Them Injuns might come back.'

'Wait,' said the redhead, he stood in a listening attitude. 'I thought I heard a groan . . . By God, yes, that one thar ain't dead.'

'You're crazy.'

But the redhead had already crossed to the body with the hideously-bleeding pate. He got down on his knees. 'Bucko,' he called. The talkative brother joined him. The dying man, who had been scalped and left for dead, was croaking something.

Bucko bent nearer. He was the least squeamish of the

four but he could not suppress a shudder. The words came
slowly, the trooper's eyes rolled with the effort. Then he
suddenly made it. Five words, one of them a name, which
brought blood to his lips then ended in the rattle of death.
But Bucko had heard them. They made his eyes blaze and
his lips tighten. '*Injuns – Renegades – Guns – Tell Burndon.*
They burnt into his brain as he realized their full terrible
portent. The name meant nothing to him but he remembered it. He rose. 'Let's ride,' he said with decision.

The others followed him. They were subdued and
silent.

As they rode away the tubby one turned his sweat-glisten-
ing face and looked back. He shuddered. The squabbling
buzzards had lined up again and were plummetting from
the sky.

'We ought to make Julesburg by nightfall,' said Bucko.
'We've suttinly got some news fer the folks thar. Whip 'em
up, boys.'

The boys needed no urging. They wanted to put as
much distance as possible between themselves and the
grizzly tableau they had just witnessed.

'See thet kinda blue haze,' said Bucko pointing.

'Yeh-Yeh.'

'That's the River Platte. It bends just over there an' I
figure Julesburg's up ahead past the bend somewhere. I
hope I'm right.'

'We hope so, too,' said his phlegmatic brother.

The palefaced tubby man seemed to be fascinated by
the sight he had just witnessed and which had upset him
so much. He kept glancing back over his shoulder, then
looking all around him, almost fearfully. It was he who
spotted the horsemen approaching to the right of them.

'White men,' he said.

'Might be them renegades the trooper spoke about,'
said Bucko. 'Keep ridin'.'

But the others were obviously intending to cut them off. There seemed about eight or nine of them. They began to wave.

'They look innocent enough,' said the lean redhead.

'Wal, I guess they're bound to ketch up with us sooner or later,' said Bucko. 'With our hosses tired an' all. We might as well slow down an' let 'em. But keep your eyes peeled and if they make any funny moves reach for your irons.'

'Shore thing.' At the mention of gunplay even the tubby man seemed to brighten up.

They jogged along nonchalantly then, as the other band came closer, reined in altogether and waited for them.

'Hi-yuh, strangers,' said one of them. They looked at him particularly and were surprised at what they saw.

He was a living skeleton – and a pretty long skeleton at that. His white cadaverous face was long, the chin and nose jutting, the teeth, long yellow and protruding, the eyes deep-sunk, glowing like polished ebony. The man was emaciated, with legs in stirrups far below the horse's body, and it was a big beast. But his rider did not look ludicrous; in a subtle way his presence was commanding, almost terrifying.

'Hi-yuh,' said the boys, almost in unison.

The skeleton's eight companions grunted greetings too. They were a villainous looking bunch. At least two of them were half-breeds. All of them affected clothing which though hardworn was better and more picturesque than the work-a-day apparel of the four young men. They looked what they were, scourings of the West, the sort that hung around the railroad and its riproaring 'line-towns' like flies round a dung-heap. The human skeleton in his subtle way was their superior yet far removed from them. His sombrero was black and unadorned, his broadcloth black and stylishly-cut . . . his two guns pearl handled.

He was speaking. 'You boys look as if you've ridden quite a way.'

'Back aways,' said Bucko briefly with a sweep of his arm.

'Come to seek your fortune in Julesburg?' said the other with a horrible grimace.

'Kinda.'

'Take them, boys,' said the other.

But Bucko had been watching and waiting. 'Look out,' he yelled and even as the villainous-looking bunch slapped leather he spurred his horse forward.

The skeleton man's draw was a thing of wonder. Bucko flung himself sideways in the saddle as the big Colt boomed. Then he was triggering himself, cursing madly as the other dodged too and out-manoeuvred him.

Guns were speaking all around now and the acrid smoke was biting and blinding to the throat and eyes. The four strangers were hemmed in. Bucko lost sight of the enemy leader and outshot a leering half-breed at point-blank range, watching the dust puff from the other's shirt, the brown hole open in his chest, the contorted mouth and glaring eyes as he fell forward across his horse's neck.

Bucko yelled like a madman as he saw his brother go down and fought to get to him. He saw Tubby fall too and Red was swaying in the saddle. Then a hot hammer smote him in the side of the head. Waves of blood seemed to leap into his eyes, rushing, then turning to black as he fell – fell . . .

TWO

There was a black whirlpool now and he was beneath it, in the middle of it, trying to break through the surface, forcing himself higher and higher. The blackness got slowly lighter and the agony got worse as he forced the water aside with his head and it buffetted and stung him in retaliation. It got suddenly lighter and he thought he had broken through. He opened his eyes to see if it was so. The light was the sun, glaring, pitiless, making him shut his eyes again. Then to open them slowly crack by crack to the sickening, searing agony of being alive once more.

He was lying on his back. He rolled on his side and lay there retching for a second or so. The pain and sickness receded a little though the hammer still thudded in his head where the bullet had ploughed a furrow. Half-an-inch lower and he'd have been dead instead of just 'creased'.

He rose to his hands and knees and began to crawl. He found his brother first. Lafe was dead. Bucko had known it was pretty useless to hope. He turned away silently and found himself looking into the staring eyes of Red; a hole above the right one and a dried red thread. Tubby was further away. He had evidently made a run for it. He had been shot about six times in the back.

Horror seized the young man. He rose to his feet and

15

began to stagger blindly away. The sun beat down on him, his feet weaved fantastic patterns in the dust, the buzzards squabbled above, cheated by this dead man who walked and babbled to himself. That was how he was when the buffalo hunters found him and he dragged out his gun and began to blaze away. They rode down on him and their leader bent in the saddle and felled him with a blow of his hand.

He cursed and fought them as they dismounted and bent over him, until they put a rolled coat beneath his head and forced whiskey down his throat. Then reason slowly came back to his blazing eyes; he sighed and became quiet.

'Take it easy, partner,' said the leader of the buffalo-hunters. 'You're among friends now.'

Bucko looked up into a lean, handsome face adorned by a moustache and imperial. He said: 'Thanks, pardner. I'm sorry I cut up rough. Me an' my brother an' our two pards got drygulched back aways. The others are dead . . . An' the train . . . Injuns . . . All soldiers murdered . . . scalped . . . Renegades . . .' He was beginning to babble again.

'Help me to get him on a horse,' said the tall bearded leader.

They lifted him up into the saddle and tied him to the beast. They wound a cloth round his head.

With the jolting rhythm of the horse beneath him, the jingling of harness in his ears, he sank into unconsciousness once more.

He regained consciousness to stinging pain in his head. Somebody was bathing the open scalp wound. It was the tall man with the moustache and imperial, which made him look like a French dandy from New Orleans. But he was more manly; bronzed, lean, tough-looking, a real man of the plains.

'What do we call you, friend,' he said.

'Jim Martin – back where I came from everybody calls me Bucko on account I'm a bronc-buster.'

'My name's Cody,' said the other. 'Bill Cody.'

'Glad tuh know yuh, Mr Cody.'

'Bill 'ull do.' The tall man turned his head. 'Boys, I want you to meet Mr Bucko Martin.'

They crowded around the dark, heavily built young man as he squatted on the ground and Cody wrapped a fresh bandage round his head. They greeted him cheerily, trying to make him forget the horror he had experienced – horror with which they themselves were very familiar.

'Where you from, Bucko?' said one.

'Down in the Pecos.'

'My, you've come quite a way.'

'Don't talk if you don't feel like it, Bucko,' said Cody as he finished tying the bandage.

'Thanks, Bill,' said the young waddy. Then: – 'No, I want to talk now – get it all off muh chest. There's a lot o' things I gotta remember – a lotta things I don't understand.'

'I've sent some o' my boys back after those skunks,' said Cody. 'But I don't hold out much hopes. They'll have flitted by now. The boys'll bring in the bodies of your brother an' friends.'

'There's the train too. Wrecked. All the soldiers scalped.'

'Yes, I know,' said Cody gently. 'It happens like that. Nobody can do anything about it. There ain't enough people to go after the Injuns. It'd just mean another massacre if they did. We got attacked the other day and lost three men. The only thing to do was fight 'em off then make a break fer it.'

'The soldier who spoke before he died said something about renegades and rifles and he said tell somebody – but

I can't remember the name. I can't remember . . .'

'Don't fret about it. It'll come back.' Cody pursed his lips. 'If these are renegade whites running with the Injuns an' supplying 'em with rifles that's bad – mighty bad. There's gonna be hell to pay when this news gets back to Julesburg. That troop of soldiers was being sent for guards on the rail-road. The men are being harried all the time they're workin' – they lose two or three every day. They're threat-ening to strike. I guess you can't blame 'em. Lots of 'em are Micks from back East. They ain't used to the country. They came out here to work not fight.'

Cody rose. Bucko rose unsteadily with him. They stood side by side. The buffalo-hunter topped Bucko's broad five feet eight by at least five inches. He was as straight as an arrow-shaft. His long brown hair hung over his shoulders. He was somewhat of a dandy but the way he wore his gun, low down on his thigh, betokened he was a dangerous one, to boot. 'Describe the men who attacked you, Bucko,' he said.

'The leader was the only one I took a great lot of notice of,' said the cowhand. 'I've never seen a *hombre* like him before. He looked like a skeleton.'

'A skeleton!' echoed Cody. 'There's only one man in these parts who looks like that an' that's Death Ordey. I might've known it . . .'

'Death Ordey,' echoed Bucko.

'Yes, nobody knows his real first name. They call him Death because that's the way he looks.'

'He suttinly does.'

Cody was hesitant. He said. 'Maybe if you told me all of it. From the beginning I mean . . .'

'Sure,' said Bucko tonelessly. It was easy to talk to this tall cavalier-like *hombre*. He looked a square shooter. Maybe if he told him everything right from the start, things would seem easier.

He told of how he and his brother, Lafe, and their two pards, Tubby and Red got tired of being Texas saddle-tramps, riding herd, breaking-in wild horses, dodging from ranch to ranch, selling their hands and their guns for peanuts, and decided to travel further afield and seek better pickings. They had heard of work that could be got easily with this new railroad that was straddling the Middle West, of big money that could be earned by a good gunnie who didn't mind trouble. Bucko had travelled this territory during the war, he knew it pretty well. He persuaded the others and took the leadership.

'If I hadn't I guess they'd've bin alive now,' he said, 'busting broncs back in the Pecos or maybe New Mexico – Lafe wanted tuh go there. He was agin this trip right from the start. But he allus finished up by doin' as I said – me bein' the eldest. An' now, 'cos o' me, he's finished. Maybe it'd been better if I'd gone with him back there . . .'

'These things happen,' said Cody softly.

'Yeh, I guess so. I'm a trouble-shooter. I allus have bin. You'd be better tuh steer clear o' me, Bill. I'm a jinx.'

'Quit bellyin' and go on with your story,' the other told him.

In the distance the sun glinted on the sluggish waters of the Platte and a dull light came into Bucko's eyes as he stared at nothingness and told of how he and the other three had found the wrecked train, the massacred soldiers, the one who spoke before he died, that name he could not remember – his face was anguished . . . Cody hurried him over this part and he told of the meeting with Death, the living skeleton, and his men and of their treachery.

'But why?' he burst out. 'What had we done to them? We were hardly worth robbin' . . .' He fumbled suddenly beneath his belt. 'They didn't even take my money.'

'Death likes killing,' said Cody. 'He's a human wolf

preying on the railroad and all around it.' His voice became thoughtful. 'An' ain't it possible that he and his men were the very same renegades who rode with the Injuns? Maybe they wanted to shut your mouths in case you'd discovered somethin'.'

'Maybe,' said Bucko dully. 'Yeh, I guess that's the only explanation.' He turned directly to the other man. 'I gotta get that Death *hombre*, Bill,' he said.

'Yes, I know.' Cody squeezed his shoulder with a sinewy hand. 'You can count me in on that, pardner. An' the rest o' the boys. How're you feelin' now?'

'Better, thanks.'

'We'll see about moving on for Julesburg then.'

As Cody turned away Bucko looked around him for the first time. While he and the leader had been talking others of the band had been finishing their job of cutting up the buffalo meat that was piled in the three canvas-covered wagons together with the hides. The hunters had had a good haul and an easy trip. But their jubilance, callous though they were, was subdued now by their awareness of Bucko and his sadness, and their thoughts of the train massacre. Not the first one, but probably the worst yet. And to think that white men had been mixed up in it, had probably planned it. That was a stink in the nostrils of all.

'Let's get movin', boys,' called Cody.

'Wait a minute, Bill,' said one of the others. 'This looks like the boys comin' back with the buckboard.'

Everybody shaded their eyes. 'It's them all right.'

The little band with the buckboard in the centre of them, galloped nearer, and finally stopped in a cloud of dust.

A huge man whose face was almost entirely hidden by masses of curly black hair was in the forefront. He screeched, pulling his startled horse up on her hind legs.

'We ran into a small Crow war-party,' he said. 'We give

'em a drubbin' to larn 'em a lesson. Killed five of 'em. An' nary a scratch between us. I got me a top-knot.'

He indicated his belt from which dangled a greasy black scalp. The blood still dripped from it on to his grimed trousers and the silky flanks of his horse.

'You're a black-hearted coyote, Dragon,' said Cody. 'Did yuh do all I told you?'

'Yeh.' Dragon's manner was a little more subdued as he indicated the buckboard and its burden covered by a voluminous horse-blanket.

'The Injuns hadn't got there first had they?'

Dragon shook his head. 'We went down to the line as well,' he said. 'Nary a sign except the usual ones. Them red devils certainly made a good job.'

Bucko had come up beside Cody. He said: 'Have they got my brother an' . . .'

'Yes, it's all right, Bucko.'

'Thanks, Bill.'

'Little a man can do,' said Cody brusquely, brutally. 'Sometimes I wish I had enough guts to take scalps like some of the oldsters here do. I guess they get a certain satisfaction . . .'

It was almost sundown when they reached the shining ribbons of the Union Pacific Railway close to Julesburg. Here was the end of the track where burly labourers laid ties and drove spikes, sweating like demons in the sun, adding yard by yard to the ribbons of steel. Hard-faced section bosses paced up and down with rifles in the crooks of their arms and at intervals troopers stood with fixed bayonets.

Cody told Bucko: 'The Injuns raided this section day before yesterday. Killed four men then vanished again like dust puffs. The place's pitifully guarded. That's what that train load of soldiers was for.'

He turned in the saddle and addressed his men. 'Keep your mouths shut all of you.'

'Sure, Bill.'

At the sight of the meat party the workers downed tools and, with shouted greetings surged forward.

'They've been short o' vittles the last couple of weeks,' said Cody. 'A meat-party got themselves cut to pieces. You see the trains are drivin' the buffaloes further afield all the time. They're mighty timid critturs. We have to go right into Injuns country to hunt 'em. I guess the red devils have got plenty o' scores against us. I guess you can't exactly blame 'em. We're driving their food away; an' chasing it an' killing it, too.'

The workers, men in sweat-soaked shirts or no shirts at all, milled nearer.

'Look at 'em,' said Cody. 'Bare-backed. An' they wonder why they keel over with sunstroke. You can't larn 'em nothing.' He rose in his stirrups. 'There's enough bully here to feed the whole of Julesburg,' he yelled.

'Good old Bill,' they cheered.

Bucko noted that the buffalo-hunters kept in a close ring around the buckboard so that timid eyes should not pry. He thought of what lay under that rough blanket and his eyes stung, his veins turned to ice.

Close at hand a huge Irishman raised his bull-like voice. 'Good f'r you, Billy ye spalpeen. All we want now is some money an' we'll be sitting pretty.' A chorus of catcalls greeted this pronouncement.

Cody said to Bucko: 'They got a mite of wages owing 'em. I hope the powers-that-be weren't crazy enough to send the gold on that train with the soldiers. If they did them renegades have got it for sure.'

Bucko nodded dully. He appreciated the tall buffalo-man's attempt to make him forget. But what was it to him if Mick labourers went without food and money. A skull-like face danced in a mirage before his eyes and his hand closed involuntarily over the butt of his gun. The murdering devils hadn't even bothered to take that.

The men had spotted the bloody scalp at Dragon's belt and were inspecting it, touching the greasy black locks gingerly with their fingers.

'You've had trouble then?' said one of them.

'Nah,' said Dragon. He spat copiously. 'Jest a war-party. We wiped 'em up.'

'An I reckon as soon as you've gone they'll come back an' take it out on us,' said another voice plaintively.

'Aw quit your squawking,' said Dragon scornfully. 'You don't have to go out in the middle of 'em like we do. I never seed such a lily-livered bunch of grandmothers.'

'Who's lily-livered?' bawled the big Irish labourer.

The bearded Dragon bowed ironically. 'Savin' your presence, Mick me boyo.'

'Bah!' said Mick.

'I wish they were all like him,' said Cody. 'Him an' Dragon are a match for any four Injuns apiece. But a lot of the workers are dead scared – more by the look o' the savages an' their screechin' than anything else I guess. I guess they ain't used to 'em like we are. That'll come with time.'

Bucko nodded dully again. Cody rose in his stirrups again. 'Back to work, ye spalpeens!' he bawled.

The Irishmen, and there were many of them in the crowd, greeted this mimicing of their own particular idiom with yells of derision.

'Break it up,' bawled the section bosses.

The meat party moved through and on to Julesburg. Julesburg, the latest line camp; 'Hell on Wheels,' the lustiest, wickedest railroad-town in Western history. This outpost of the civilized States spearing into the land of the red man was the last word in vice, organized and otherwise.

It was dark when the meat-party reached it; the lights were blazing from the big tents and the clapboard buildings. The liquor was already beginning to run, the pianos to clank, the fiddles to scrape; the dance-hall girls and whores were preening themselves to receive the customers. The shifting metropolis of the old U.P. was beginning to pop again. The gamblers shot their cuffs and, pale-faced and hard-eyed, waited for the suckers.

'Dragon!' bawled Cody.

'Yeh, boss.'

'Take over.'

'Right, boss.'

Cody turned to Bucko. 'Come with me,' he said. 'I'll fix you up at Mother Brannigan's. What you want right now is a real load of shut-eye.'

'How about—' Bucko winced as he indicated the buck-board.

'My men'll take it to the undertaking parlour. You can't do nothin' now, Bucko. Come with me.'

The half-dazed cowboy suffered himself to be led away by the tall soldierly buffalo-man.

The rooming-house Cody had mentioned proved to be a two-storey frame building with a rickety veranda. As they climbed the steps the tall swashbuckler said: 'Mother Brannigan runs a whorehouse on the side. It's down the street a piece. But she's got a heart o' gold. She don't allow women in this place – the only female here besides herself is Minnie Crow, she's a half-breed an' deaf and dumb. She carries a knife in her stockin'. The other week a teamster tried to give her a tumble. She punctured him right thru' the liver. He cashed-in his chips a couple of days later.'

'Nice people,' commented Bucko without humour.

'You'll get used to 'em.'

'Yeh, I will. I guess some o' the shebangs along the Rio Grande are jest as bad. I've seen 'em all.'

Bucko was jerked out of his grief-ridden lethargy by the sight of Mother Brannigan. She was one of the largest women he had ever seen and definitely the ugliest. He almost laughed when Cody told him she had buried three husbands and was now living with a Scotch barman little more than half her size. Her fat hung on her, shapeless like blubber; in her long voluminous skirt of a filthy and indefinite hue, she looked like a huge sack filled with wet mud. But her face was the worst. To Bucko it seemed even bigger than that of the hairy monster, Dragon. It had hair, too; a quite prominent black moustache and a few curly tendrils distributed pretty evenly over three sagging chins. Mother Brannigan had a nose like a pounded hunk of putrid meat and her eyes were so sunk in folds of yellowish flesh that they looked like little glittering black currants. She leered, revealing a huge mouthful of brown uneven teeth.

'Wal, if it ain't my ol' sweetheart Buff'ler Bill Cody.'

'Hallo, Ma,' said the tall man and with magnificent aplomb caught the old woman's fat, grimy hand, made a stately bow and kissed it.

'Bill,' said Ma, and she simpered. It was worse than her toothy leer.

Cody introduced Bucko. The old woman took the young cowboy's hand in a grip that swallowed it and made him wince. Cody didn't dwell on his new friend's sorrows right then but said: 'You can find Bucko a room can't you?'

'Sure thing.'

And a room he had: a low dark room with a small window that looked out on the rubbish-dumps of Julesburg. It was fairly clean, and the bed, though lumpy, was pretty soft. Cody left almost immediately after telling Bucko when he had rested sufficiently to meet him at the Palladin Eating House. Bucko took off his gunbelt, his boots and his chaps and lay down on the bed. His mind was one big question-mark across which danced a skull-like face; while behind it all a name hammered to be admitted, in vain. If only he could remember that name . .. if only he could get a lead on Death Ordey. If only . . . If! If! If! Cody had left him. He was lost and alone in the darkness. The dead faces of his brother and his two pard-ners mocked him and a skeleton with a gun lurked nearby. Instrumental accompaniment was supplied by squabbling turkey-buzzards and screeching Indians.

Then above it all, voices began to chant loudly: 'You killed us. You killed us,' and the three dead faces grimaced and glared.

THREE

The roaring night of Julesburg was well under way when he awoke with a bitter mouth and a thumping head, lapping on the fringes of the nightmare and coming to full consciousness with a terrible sense of frustration. If only he could get to grips with something. He remembered he had promised to meet Cody somewhere, but he could not remember the name of the place, that was another question mark in his mind: had that knock on the head muddled-up his faculties?

He climbed out of bed. He felt dizzy and the pain banged in his head as if it would drive him down again. With a superhuman effort he kept on his feet and tottered over to the wash-basin. He splashed his face with stale, icy water. He couldn't find a towel so he wiped himself on his bandanna. He struggled into his boots, strapped on his chaps (he felt lost without them) and buckled on his gunbelt with the forty-five in the low hanging sheath tied to his thigh with a whang-string. He clapped his Stetson on his head and winced. He guessed it looked kind of funny perched on top of the bandages, but he would feel half-undressed if he went out without it.

Already he felt better. He tried a practice-draw. The leering face of Death Ordey loomed up in front of him and he almost thumbed the hammer. He shrugged as he

27

reholstered his gun. He mustn't get the willies. What he had to do in the Platte country would need a cool head and a quick brain – unless he wanted to finish up like Lafe, Red and Tubby. He winced again, with inward pain this time. He must stop dwelling on it . . . Action! Action!

His step was steadier and more purposeful as he descended the stairs. Mother Brannigan was nowhere in sight. Probably she was at the other establishment Cody had told him about, Bucko reflected. He hadn't forgotten that. But he had forgotten the name of the place where he was to meet the buffalo-man.

A pasty-faced youth was sitting behind the table which, placed in the corner of the lobby, served as a desk for the rooming-house. Bucko went across to him and explained his predicament. The youth eyed him with suspicion.

'Is it the Jackman Hotel?' he said at length.

'Nope.'

'Maybe it'd be the Palladin Eatin' House then. That's where the Buff'ler has most of his meals.'

The cowboy's sombre eyes lit up for a second. 'That's it,' he said. 'Thanks a heap, pardner. How do I get to it?'

'Jest down the street a piece. On the same side of the road. There's a sign – you can't miss it.'

'Thanks, pardner.'

The youth had thawed out. 'Don't mention it,' he said.

But with a speculative eye he watched the broad, dark bow-legged young man sway out on high-heeled riding-boots. He looked like a gunman. Who was he? What had he to do with Bill Cody?

The Palladin Eating House was packed to its sagging swing doors. All the tables were occupied and people were standing about with sandwiches and mugs of coffee in their fists. Amid curses, some good-natured, many vicious, Bucko wormed his way through the press and looked for his friend.

He didn't seem to be anywhere around. Finally, Bucko asked a grinning teamster if he had seen him.

'Will Cody? Yeh. He went out about ten minutes ago.'

'Thanks.'

'You're welcome, stranger.' The teamster eyed him speculatively as he turned away. Then forgot him.

Bucko bought coffee and a meat sandwich (already Bill's buffaloes seemed to have been put to good use) from the little puddled bar, and joined the standing throng.

He looked around him again, covertly eyeing his neighbours. They were a feeding multitude whose variety made him almost dizzy. Scouts and buffalo-hunters with wide hats and buckskin clothes, many frayed and beaded like Indians; high-booted teamsters and uniformed troopers; black garbed, cold-eyed gamblers and professional gunmen; storekeepers; labourers; half-breeds and Indians in blanket-coats or capes very like the serapes worn along the Rio Grande; whores and dance-hall girls taking time off from their labours; Pawnee scouts, brothers to the paleface, hereditary enemies of the Sioux and Cheyennes ... what a whirling, babbling conglomeration of lusty life, laughter and wickedness. Even in the cosmopolitan border towns of Texas, New Mexico and Arizona Bucko had never seen such a variety of coloured humanity. Then he spotted a huge hairy figure ploughing through the mob towards him, knocking people right and left. But nobody cursed the Dragon.

He came to a stop in front of Bucko, towering above him.

'Howdy, son.'

'Hallo, Dragon. I'm lookin' fer Cody. D'yuh know where he is?'

'That's what I came here to tell yer. He tol' me to look out for yer an' tell yer to hang on here. He'll be back pretty soon.'

'All right, thanks.'

'How's the noodle?' said Dragon.

'Almost good as new now, I guess.'

'I knew you wasn't a lily-white,' boomed the giant. 'What er y' aimin' to do now?'

Bucko patted his gun. 'I got plenty o' work fer muh Colt to do ef'n I can find out where it is.'

'I get you,' said Dragon. Then: – 'Well, if ever you need any help, son – any scragging or scalping ter do, I'm yer man.' His terrific booming laugh rang out, and people turned and grinned. In this town of characters Dragon was one unique.

He squeezed Bucko's arm, making the young man wince. 'Well, son, I gotta leave yer. I gotta go see my woman.' Beneath the black hair that sprouted in all directions from his huge face his tobacco-stained jagged teeth showed in a leer. He winked one bloodshot eye. Then with another squeeze he turned away. Taking no chances, the crowd parted to let him through.

Bucko watched him go and wondered what his woman was like. The only female he had seen that could conceivably be a match for the huge buffalo-hunter was Mother Brannigan. He learnt later that Dragon kept a massive Crow squaw and a 'passel of papooses' in a tent just outside town – although some of the town-whores bragged about accommodating him too.

Another hunter from Cody's party came over to Bucko. A wiry, ferret-faced man who cursed a lot. They talked desulatorily. Then suddenly the man said: 'Here's Bill. I'll be leavin' you.' He sidled off.

The leader joined Bucko. 'How're you feelin' now?'

'Fine, Bill.'

'That's good,' Cody's voice was low. 'I fixed the buryin' for tomorrow.'

'Thanks, Bill.'

Cody ignored it and muttered on. 'News o' the train massacre is all over town now. It'd got to be sooner or later. The workers are getting jittery – they always do when anything like that happens. The worst part of it is that a lot of them think their wages were on that train and the renegades took 'em. Personally, I don't think so. If it is so it certainly is a big advantage for the other side.'

'The other side?' echoed the cowboy.

'Maybe that's speaking a bit wildly,' said Cody. 'But you must understand, Bucko, there are hundreds of people out here, and back East, who don't want the U.P. to get thru' an' are doing all they can to stop it. People peddling liquor to the savages – have been doin' fer years – now they're having a job to get it thru'. Now on top of that there's this tale about the Injuns getting rifles, and renegades to lead 'em. All this, the orders an' the stuff, come from back East. And we can't get a line on any of the people behind it all.' In his indignation the buffalo-hunter was a little agitated.

'I suspect Death Ordey of being the big man this end in the liquor smuggling. He's wanted for plenty of other things, too. He's been a thorn in our side along the Platte for quite a spell. He's clever, he works with the Indians and hides himself well. We've scoured the territory for him more than once but he just seems to vanish.'

As Cody talked Bucko figured the tall soldierly man must be something more in the Platte country than just a buffalo-hunter.

Cody continued: 'I've never known of Death and his boys riding with the Injuns, altho' he's pally with them. But it's quite possible. I wouldn't be surprised if some of his men weren't the renegades that the dyin' trooper spoke about. He tried to tell you something . . .'

'I wish I could remember that name!' said Bucko.

'It'll come back,' said Cody. 'Maybe it ain't important anyway.'

He stretched himself and yawned, a supple picture of health.

'I've just been to see General Casement an' old Judge Mackey. Casement's the contractor-general for the U.P. A good scout. The judge's an irritable old cuss. But he means well. He's done a helluva lot to help bring law along the Platte.' He grinned mirthlessly. 'Not so's you'd notice . . . I told them about you. Everything. They want to meet you. They want me to take you down there. Right now if you like. May mean a job, Bucko, a chance to get what you want – to get back at Death Ordey an' all his kind.'

'All right,' said the young cowboy. 'What are we waiting for? Come on.'

Cody led him down the street, bright as day with the light streaming from the establishments along its cart-rutted length. Most of the lights were behind them when the tall man pushed aside the flap of a large tent and ushered Bucko inside.

Three men sat behind a long table littered with papers. They rose.

'This is the young man I told you about, gentlemen,' said Cody.

'Bucko Martin – meet General Casement.'

The cowboy shook hands with the lean red-bearded man, who eyed him keenly.

'Judge Mackey.'

The judge was bent and old but his blue eyes snapped like fire crackers. And his grip was still good.

'Ralph Burndon.'

As Bucko gripped the hand of the fair-headed, moustached man who was stylishly dressed in broadcloth and a silk cravat, something clicked in his mind. That name! It sounded familiar.

Burndon grinned, showing white even teeth. Bucko

grinned back, nonchalantly at ease, although his brain was seething.

'Sit down gentlemen,' said General Casement. He reached for the decanter and glasses at his elbow and poured drinks. As the two men seated themselves he passed them a glass of wine each. 'This is good stuff.' He raised his own glass. 'Your health, gentlemen.'

They sipped. Bucko was not impressed. He wanted to get down to cases. He was aware that all three men were eyeing him keenly across the table.

'Sorry to hear about your loss, son,' said the General suddenly.

'Thank you, suh.'

'We'd like you to tell us, if you will, all you know about the train massacre. Will Cody's already told us, but we'd like to hear it from your own lips in case he missed something.'

'I'd be glad, suh.' Bucko liked this man's straightforward manner.

He launched into his tale; with repetition the horrors were beginning to pall, he was becoming a whole man once more. When he got to the point where the dying soldier spoke to him all three men seemed to listen more intently.

'The dying man told you a name and you don't remember it?' said Judge Mackey querulously.

'Yeh.' Bucko said. 'I guess this knock on the haid didn't do me a whole heap o' good. The soldier said "tell somebody . . ." but who – I can't remember. I guess it'll come back to me.'

'Did the soldier give you anything?' said General Casement.

'No.'

'Did you search him?'

'No . . . I ain't seen very many scalped men, General. I

guess I didn't think of it. There didn't seem no reason to anyway.' Bucko wondered why they attached so much importance to the babblings of a dying trooper. They had seemed important to him at first but were not so much now. Death Ordey was the man he wanted to know about.

The four men exchanged glances full of meaning. Bill Cody said: 'I'll vouch for Bucko, gentlemen. I'd like to have him with us.'

Then Ralph Burndon spoke up. 'Mr Martin . . . this name the trooper used. Was it by any chance my name? Burndon. Did he say "tell Burndon"?'

'Burndon,' echoed Bucko. 'Somethin' like that. Yeh, I guess it was.'

The blond man shrugged. 'He didn't mention another name did he?'

'Nope, only that one.'

'You might as well tell him,' said Cody.

'All right,' said General Casement. 'But you understand, Mr Martin, this is between ourselves. Nobody else knows the full circumstances.'

'Sure, suh,' said Bucko.

Judge Mackey grunted, whether in agreement or not was hard to determine.

'*You'd* better tell him, Burndon,' said Casement.

'All right,' the blond man looked at Bucko. 'Mr Martin, that dying soldier who spoke to you was no ordinary trooper. He was an agent for the government – investigating liquor peddling. He got a line on the people back East who were responsible and followed up the trail. He was to return here in the guise of a trooper with, we hoped, the names of the ringleaders back East and also here along the Platte. Bill Cody's been working on it this end. He says everything points to Death Ordey as being the king-pin here. But catching Ordey is a different matter. Bill runs a sort of unofficial vigilantes band, all his trusted buffalo-hunters are in it and a few of the trustworthy railwaymen. If you want to join up with them . . .'

'I suttinly do,' said Bucko.

'Now you tell us, Mr Martin, that renegades are running with the Indians and the red devils are using rifles too.'

'That's what I gathered from what the trooper said.'

'That means they're getting organized,' said Burndon. 'That's bad. The railroad has got to keep moving or the powers-that-be will quit subsidising it. There are powerful people working against us, Mr Martin – we wished we knew who they are – people to whom progress means less profit. People who'd sooner sell rot-gut whiskey and firearms to Indians than help their country. They don't think the railroad'll get thru'. And if its left to them it won't . . . If we'd got a couple of hundred Texan gunmen like you, if you don't mind my saying so, Mr Martin, we'd be damn sight happier men.'

'Wal, here's one you can count on, suh. An' there'd've been three more ef . . .'

'I was coming to that,' said Burndon hastily. 'Why did Death Ordey and his men shoot at you? I guess the only reason could be that they wanted to silence you in case you had learned something at the wreck – or because they didn't want you to bring the news to Julesburg right away.

'Mr Cody an' me figured somethin' like that,' said Bucko.

The tall buffalo-man nodded grimly. Then he said: 'Gentlemen, I'd like to get as many men as I can and go out after Ordey.'

'It's risky, Will,' said General Casement. 'You'd probably have to go right into the heart of Indian country. You couldn't get enough men from Julesburg to hold a big Indian raid.'

'Yes, it's a risk,' said Cody. 'But it's better than kicking our heels around here. I've brought enough meat in to last quite a spell. But we could go out masquerading as another meat-party. I'd take volunteers only and make sure they were people I know and can trust.'

Casement shrugged. 'It's up to you, Will,' he said. He smiled in the midst of his red beard. 'I guess if you want to go, there isn't much any of us can do about it.'

Bucko spoke up then. 'Here's your first volunteer, Bill.'

Cody clapped him on the shoulder. 'You're taken . . . There are one or two things to do in town first,' he added soberly. 'An' then we'll ride.'

General Casement stuck out his hand. 'Well, I've got to go back along the line first thing tomorrow morning so I'll wish you boys luck.'

Both of them shook the old soldier's hand then, in their turns, the old judge's gnarled one and Ralph Burndon's strong well-kept paw. They left the tent.

There was a press in the street outside one of the larger honky-tonks. In the glare that came from the cracked windows of the ramshackle frame building a man was standing on a box and bawling at the top of his voice. As they got nearer they could hear what he said. It went something like this:

'Ladies an' gennelmen. Fellow workers. Are we goin' to keep bein' trod on, stamped inter the ground by the employees of fat-bellied Easterners who're making millions out of this yere railroad? While we sweat an' toil, fight Injuns, starve, get kilt. No money. No help from nobody. These fat pigs wallow with their wimmin in silk and ermine an' swill champagne . . .'

'Quite a speechmaker,' said Cody.

The rambling discourse went on . . . 'Now the train's bin wrecked an' a lot of brave sojer-lads brutally massacred. An' our wages gone with 'em. Are we going to keep on workin' fer people who won't send no real troops out to guard us? Ef'n there'd been more sojers on that train they'd've got thru'. Only a handful of 'em there was. Are we going to stand fer it I say? Down tools I say, every manjack – an' the wimmin too . . .' His voice was drowned by the roar of laughter that greeted this last sally.

But there were more ominous cries too. Many of the crowd were taking the half-drunken orator as seriously as he took himself. There were cries of 'Strike! Strike!' 'Damn the railroad.' 'Money-grabbin' swine' and other phrases of a like nature.

Cody shook his head. 'I guess they have got a grievance at that,' he said. 'They were promised a lot when they came – in particular, protection. Nobody can say they're getting it. I hope this mob don't get out of hand. If he means to stir up trouble that speechifier sure has the right idea. I wonder if he's a genuine worker who conscientiously figures he's been ill-used or whether he's jest a mouthpiece for somebody else. I can't recollect ever seeing him before . . .'

'Let's stop him at it then,' said Bucko.

Cody shook his head once more. 'That'd probably do more harm than good. He ain't the first hot-air gent I've seen on this street. Right now I think the majority here are just havin' a laugh . . .'

'How about those who're yelling?'

'Probably partners o' the one on the box.'

The man was still yapping, reiterating everything that he had already said although owing to the fact that some-body had passed him a bottle of liquor, it was even more garbled than before. The crowd began to jeer.

'See what I mean?' said Cody. 'It's a good job they've got full bellies . . .' His voice sobered. 'I hope the town's a whole lot clearer tomorrow mornin' when they bring them poor slaughtered troopers in.'

'Ain't nobody bin down there . . . ?'

'That'd be suicide, at night. The Platte's swarming with scalp-hunting Injuns. Nothing can hurt 'em any more anyway. A night out won't hurt 'em. Come on, let's get thru' here.'

FOUR

Cody began to make a passage through the throng. Bucko followed him. A painted woman who was screeching with laughter suddenly caught hold of his arm saying, 'Can I help ya out, pretty-boy?'

'Not tonight, ma'am,' said the cowboy.

'Aw, c'mon.'

'No, thanks.' Bucko tried to snatch his arm away but she clung on, her nails digging into his muscle.

'Gee, you're strong,' she said. 'C'mon. The night air's bad fer me. Come on inside.'

Cody, unaware of the incident, was forging onwards.

'I got business,' said Bucko and literally threw the jade away from him.

Right here seemed to be the noisiest and most quarrelsome section of the crowd.

'Whose this stranger who's pushing our Sal around?' bawled a big workman and launched himself at Bucko.

Ready to meet any prospect of action more than halfway the cowboy struck out. His fist connected with a satisfying smack to the side of the man's jaw. The fellow was precipitated back into the thick of the crowd. Then he was shoved back into Bucko's arms, only to stop another blow that had been aimed at Bucko from behind. The young man let the other drop to the floor and turned.

Another blow, hitting its intended target this time smote his shoulder and spun him around. As he was tottering he parried another thrust and kicked out with a booted foot. A man yowled in agony. Next moment Bucko was in the middle of a glorious free-for-all. His original opponent was screeching in the dust beneath heavy spiked boots. Bucko looked around for another one and received a smack flush in the mouth that sent him backwards, brought salt blood to his mouth, and made his senses swim.

He recovered himself, the press of the shuffling, shouting people holding him on his feet. He struck out blindly, hit something soft and let out a wild Texan 'yippee'! Then he found himself indulging in a slogging-match with a lantern-jawed teamster.

A terrific blow caught him high in the head, plomb on his wound. The pain blinded and sickened him. He felt himself falling into blackness and began to grope.

He thought he heard, faintly, like an echo, a fusillade of shots. Then strong hands caught hold of him, dragged him, stood him up straight against a wall. He shook his head to dispel the fog, opened his eyes, and looked into the face of Bill Cody.

'I'm mighty indebted to you, Mr Cody,' he said owlishly. 'You keep savin' my bacon.'

'You need a wet nurse,' the other said drily.

They stood on the boardwalk outside a honky-tonk. The crowd was pretty still. In the heat of the battle somebody had drawn a gun. A man staggered into the open and fell face-down in the dust. Others picked him up. He had been shot in the stomach. They carried him into the honky-tonk.

'That's how most fights finish around here,' said Cody. 'If it ain't a shooting its a stabbing. Offtimes it's the workers that start it. It's always a good excuse for some light-fingered gent to put paid to somebody he ain't fond of.'

'That old whore started it all,' said Bucko.

'Women!' Cody spat. 'They cause as much trouble as the U.P. an' the Injuns.'

At signs of trouble the soapbox orator seemed to have vanished. The crowd split up and began to trickle back into the places of amusement.

As the swing-doors flapped to behind the bunch who carried the shot man, Cody said: 'He's either dead or he ain't.' He spiced his cavalier manner with such spasms of brutal levity; that was the epitome of Julesburg. He said: 'Come on, let's go to Mother Brannigan's and I'll fix that head of yours again.'

The head in question definitely needed further treatment, the edges of the bandage were dyed with fresh crimson.

The old madam was back at her post and desirous of knowing what all the ruckus was about.

Cody told her. 'How about rustlin' up some fresh bandage an' stuff for Bucko?'

'Sure thing. Get on up. I'll bring it to you.'

The two men went up to Bucko's room. Bill's own cubby – he always stayed with Mother Brannigan when he was in town – was along at the other end of the landing.

Presently the fat ugly old dame came in with a bowl of boiling water, and enough bandages, lint etc., to accommodate a regiment.

Cody's strong deft fingers soon made a sturdy job of work on the cowboy's battered pate. Then the buffalo-hunter said: 'Now lie down on that bed an' get some rest. I don't want you sick on my hands. I've got to go out again fer a bit . . .'

'Wal, Bill, I . . .'

'Do as I say,' said Cody with mock sternness. 'If you want to come a-ridin' with me an' the boys you've got to be fit. It'll be no picnic you know.'

Bucko became subdued. 'All right,' he said and lay down on the bed.

He heard Cody's sharp steps clatter down the stairs and fade away. He figured he certainly owed a lot to the tall buffalo-man. Despite his rather dandified curly moustache and pointed imperial Bill Cody was no slouch, he was a good man to have in any pinch. Bucko was mighty glad he had met up with him, mighty glad to be able to go right along with him – particularly if it meant a chance to get to grips with Death Ordey.

Steps thudded on the stairs, came along the landing. Came a knock on the door and the manlike voice of Mother Brannigan saying: 'Kin I come in, Mr Bucko?'

'Sure, Ma. Come right in.'

The huge woman came in carrying a tray with half-a-bottle of whiskey and a couple of glasses. In Bucko's eyes she looked almost beautiful now.

She said: 'I brought you a li'l night-cap an' I thought you wouldn't mind me havin' one with you. I'd sort of like to get better acquainted with Buff'ler Bill's new pardner.'

'You're mighty welcome, ma'am,' said the cowboy. 'Draw up a chair an' lets crack that thar bottle.'

Ma's moustache quivered as she grinned. The chair groaned in agony beneath her bulk. She took the bottle in her huge pads as if it were a newborn babe. She opened it and poured a couple of fingers in each glass.

She raised her own, like a splinter in her sausage-like fingers. 'Here's scalps on your belt,' she said. 'An' plenty o' women an' wealth.' It was her favourite toast, reserved for her specials.

'Mud in your gob,' said Bucko.

She tossed off her glass, then quivered horribly with silent laughter. 'You're a Texan all right,' she said as he poured himself another drink.

She took half of it and then placed the glass back on the

tray and leered at Bucko.

'I got another little place down the street,' she said.

'Yeh, I know. Bill told me.'

'Him!' snorted Ma, scornfully. 'The long-legged galoot never comes near it. It's my opinion he's got himself a coupla juicy young squaws stashed away someplace. He's always goin' off on his lonesome.'

Bucko probably had a better inkling of the meaning of Cody's lonely trips than had the old dame, but he kept his mouth shut.

'Down at my place I got some o' the purtiest gels in the 'ull territory. I kin pick out a right special one fer you, Bucko me boy.'

'Right now, Ma, I got no time fer young women,' said the cowboy gravely. 'I got other things to do.'

The old lady wagged her head soulfully. 'Yeh, I guess you have, son. Forgive me fer mentionin' it.'

'Sure. Forget it.' Bucko smiled wryly. 'I might give your little place a call later on at that.'

They swigged liquor again, then Bucko said: 'How long you known Cody, Ma?'

'Few months. He came down from the old line-camp, North Platte. It's a ghost town now, what's left of it. He stayed with me right from the start.' Mother Brannigan shook her huge, greying head again. 'He's a queer galoot is the Buff'ler. He don't play around in town much like the others. He sorta vanishes every now an' then. Still, most of these buffalo-men seem kinda crazy, goin' out in the middle o' Injun country like they do. Now look at that big galoot they call Dragon. He ain't no man, he's a half-breed grizzly-b'ar . . .'

The pot calling the pannikin black, thought Bucko wryly. He listened to Ma's half-scornful, half-appreciative tirade on the subject of the bearded Dragon, then switched the conversation again to Cody.

He learnt, as he already had guessed, that the buffalo-leader was pretty popular in Julesburg. His worst rival was another boss called 'Bitter Creek' Johnson who was temporarily laid up with a busted leg since Indians raided his meat-party and killed most of his men.

Ma didn't know a lot about Cody except that as a youth he had been a pony-express rider and he also fought in the war and was a scout for the army.

'Wal,' said Bucko. 'Fer such a young man he seems to have had quite a career.'

'Yeh,' agreed Ma. 'But if he ain't keerful he ain't gonna have no more career. You look after him, Bucko, or his scalp'll be dangling at a Sioux belt before he's much older.'

'I'll look after him, Ma,' said Bucko. 'I guess it's time I did. I owe him a heap.'

The cowboy felt a better man when he awoke the following morning. His head was a little thick, but that was probably as much due to the liquor he had drunk as to anything else. He gingerly pressed the wound beneath the bandage. His exploring fingers stabbed a sore spot and he winced. But he figured the place was healing up pretty tidily. He'd let Cody have another look at it.

He had not seen the buffalo-man again last night. He did not hear him go up to his room.

Cody was a bit of a mystery, a friendly yet aloof sort of man. Bucko reckoned the two of them were about the same age, but at times the buffalo-hunter seemed immeasurably older. At first glance the moustache and imperial and soldierly bearing made him look older; then, on greeting him, in his good-humour he was like a merry boy. Then again at times when his face was in repose, it looked stern and reserved, its smooth brownness drawn and worried, the dark eyes shadowed.

Bucko climbed into his pants, strapped the inevitable chaps atop of them. Then his gunbelt, handling it gently, the sunlight glinting on the brass caps of the shells in their little pouches. He took out his gun and hefted it in his hand, the feel of the smooth walnut butt in his rough palm gave him new confidence. A man only lived once. Some long, some short – it rested with how the cards were stacked. If your pards went and you stayed – well, maybe there was a good reason for it. And what you had to do you did . . . He deftly spun the cylinder of the Colt, scrutinized it minutely. It shone with a faint film of oil, just enough, and the shells in the cylinder winked at him. Satisfied, he slid it into its holster. He put his foot up on the bed. He caught hold of the greasy ends of the leather whang-string that dangled from the end of the sheath. He pulled them round his thigh, tied the ends round the leg of his jeans beneath the worn chaps. He crossed to the window and looked out into the morning sunshine. He felt suddenly kind of sad again. The room behind him was empty, he looked out into an alien country. It would have been so different had Lafe been at his shoulder, or Tubby or Red. Cody? Yeh, there was Cody; he was a square hombre. But he had his own pards, his own interests.

The rubbish dumps beneath his window mocked the sunlight and the wind-blown plains beyond. Bucko turned away from them: he guessed he'd go downstairs and get some eats. He opened the door and went out on to the landing. The sound of wagon-wheels in the street out front made him pause and look through the landing window.

The wagons, consisting of two flat buckboards and a couple of prairie-schooners with their canvas tops left off, passed beneath him slowly in the quiet, early dusty street. Men and women were coming out of doors all around to watch them go by, to mutter questions to the grim-faced mounted troopers who flanked them on each side.

Bucko heard somebody say: 'Did you see any o' the red devils?'

A trooper shook his head silently.

The wagons were covered flatly with tarpaulin that bulged here and there but concealed their burdens, save for a lean pallid hand dangling from the edge of one of them.

The cavalcade passed on and out of sight. The rumbling of the wheels died away. The dust shifted and lay still. Muttering among themselves the onlookers went back to their dens. Bucko turned away from the window and went downstairs.

He was having breakfast at the Palladin Eating House when the bugler blew the poignant, silver notes of the Last Post and down by the small ring of tents that was Army headquarters the Stars and Stripes fluttered slowly down to half-mast. The unsung heroes of the train massacre were being put to rest. A few minutes later the rattle of the gun salute rang out. Then there was absolute silence.

Bill Cody entered the eating-house and came over to Bucko.

'I've been down to see Jobson, the undertaker,' he said. 'It'll be eleven o'clock.'

'Thanks, Bill,' said Bucko soberly. 'I don't know what I'd do without you.'

'You'd get along.'

'It wuz mighty thoughtful of you to go down there. I wuz sorta sitting here tryin' tuh pluck up courage . . .'

'Who're you kiddin',' said the buffalo-man. 'You're no cry-baby. Anyway, it's done now. Eleven o'clock. I guess I'll have me a cup o' coffee. I came down here earlier an' had breakfast. You were snoring like billyho so I didn't disturb you. How'd you feel this morning?'

'Fine.'

'I'll have a look at that head when we get back.'

'Thanks . . . Figuring on ridin' tonight?'

'I think so. Comin' along?'

'You bet.'

Bucko finished his meal. Cody had his coffee. They smoked a cigarette apiece then went back to Mother Brannigan's. Up in Bucko's room Cody took the bandages from the cowboy's head and scrutinized the livid weal.

'It's fine,' he said. 'You can leave 'em off now if you like. The fresh air 'ull do it good.'

'Sure. Leave 'em off.' Bucko crossed to the window, lifted the sash. He rolled the dressings up into a ball and pitched it out on to the rubbish dump below.

He smoothed his hair with his hand and placed his Stetson gingerly over the wiry black locks.

'I feel fine,' he said. 'An', believe me, I won't be caught nappin' next time I meet up wi' Mr Death Ordey.'

'The time'll come,' said Cody.

It was almost eleven o'clock. They went downstairs. Mother Brannigan was in the lobby and she asked Bucko if he would mind her coming along – seeing he was kinda one of her boys now.

The cowboy said she'd be mighty welcome. She put on her poke bonnet and a voluminous, though rather moth-eaten, fur coat and went down the road with them.

At the funeral parlour they found Dragon and a dozen more of the buffalo-men, Jobson the undertaker, and a sky pilot who was generally known as Gin Rummy because of his inordinate liking for this game. He was lank, pale and garbed in black. His accents were nasally mournful. He played his part well. He would have been ludicrous if it were not for his obvious sincerity. He was a crusading spirit; Bucko figured he was a brave man to be preaching religion in a hell-hole like Julesburg.

It was a real cowboy funeral. The buffalo-men acted as bearers and carried the coffins slowly to Boot Hill. A small crowd followed the assemblage. Julesburg was pretty dead until dusk; a funeral was a diversion. Their chattering was quelled by the menacing glares turned upon them by Bill Cody and his dark, tough-looking companion. Slowly they began to drift away. There was no hearse, no black horses, no plumes. In Julesburg they were unfamiliar with the austere nobility of a cowboy funeral as exemplified by this solemn slow-pacing cavalcade.

It reached Boot Hill. The three open graves, the three simple wooden head boards were already waiting. The sunshine was benignant as the three cowboys, so far from their home land, were lowered gently to their last resting-place. The sky pilot spoke a short but sincere and moving benediction.

The cavalcade moved away again as the spadefuls of soil began to thud into the graves. The men worked quickly: they were used to burying all sorts up in this Julesburg Boot Hill. Many of them did not have coffins. As for head-boards – they were an unheard-of-luxury!

They paid no heed to the silent man who had stayed behind. He was young, dark, so broadly built that he looked stocky.

The sunlight softened the lines on his broad mahogany face so that he looked almost boyish. Back East rugged young men like him were still playing football in spacious college fields – dreaming maybe of going out West to fight the bandits and the romantic red men. That would be fun for them, or so they thought. Just like everything else in their young lives had been fun. There could be no blood-thirsty thoughts in their minds, no solemn vows such as echoed in the mind of this young Westerner standing in the lonely windswept burying ground in that outpost of the States. Julesburg – called so romantically by the Eastern press, 'Hell on Wheels.'

FIVE

It was night on the plains. The stars were high and lit the dark rolling spaces but dimly. Coyotes yelped and howled, calling to each other, squabbling; while from further away, probably up in the hills, a wolf bayed.

The horsemen travelled fast, but silently. They were used to traversing enemy country. The covered wagon in their midst was well-oiled. It's horses were being whipped to a steady gallop, the wagon swayed from side to side perilously but all it did was creak a little from time to time.

They had travelled far since sundown without a sight of anything human. But they did not relax their vigilance or their caution. Maybe they were being tracked by foxey red men right now.

As they drew nearer to the Black Hills, the baying of the wolf sounded much nearer. When they halted by a clump of cottonwoods at the base of the foothills the animal had gone silent. Nor as they dismounted, and tethered their horses, did they hear him again.

'Pesky critturs,' said Dragon. 'They give you away quicker'n smoke the way they run away at the first wind o' yuh. They sound mighty bold but they're the scareyest animals in the territory.'

'Yeh,' said Bucko Martin. 'We got 'em where I come from. Timber wolves. They might fetch down a dogie now and then if he wanders off on his lonesome. But they do no harm otherwise. They make more noise than anythin' else.'

Bill Cody joined them. 'If we find Death Ordey an' his boys – anywhere, it'll be in these hills around here some-place – altho' they bin combed before without success, an' one posse lost a couple o' scalps to the Injuns. Still, we gotta keep tryin'. We'll camp here fer tonight. No fires mind you. At dawn we'll leave the wagon and move up into the hills.'

'That shore is the best plan, Will,' said Dragon. 'If we met up with Ordey in the dark the cairds 'ud all be stacked on his side 'cos he knows these hills like his own saddle. But in the daylight we'd have a better chance.'

Mugs of cold coffee, laced with rum, were passed around and the men ate dried buffalo meat which, though leathery and lacking the juice and flavour of the fresh stuff, was mighty sustaining. Then they rolled themselves in the blankets and lay in, around and under the wagon. Bucko took first guard with three other men. When they were relieved by Dragon and some others two hours later they had not seen or heard a thing.

'I hate these dark, quiet nights,' said the action-loving Dragon. 'I a'most wish the moon 'ud come up.'

'Then we might get spotted,' said Bucko.

'Yeh, but at least we'd see 'em coming. We might've been heard already. Injuns might be crawlin' all around us like a lotta grass-hoppers.'

'Aw, quit bawlin', Dragon,' grinned another man. 'If they wuz all around us I guess we'd smell 'em.'

Bucko found a place with the big bearded buffalo-hunter beneath the wagon. He had wondered at first why Cody had insisted on bringing the cumbersome vehicle along. But the leader explained to him that Ordey was sure to have spies in or around Julesburg. If they saw a wagon going out they'd figure it was just another meat-party. Whereas a bunch of heavily-armed horsemen might cause them to speculate and ride to their boss with the news.

'There's enough ammunition an' stuff in there to start a war,' he said. 'There's more than one scoutin'-party bin slaughtered because they ran out o' the necessary.'

Bucko awoke with somebody shaking his shoulder. It was Dragon.

'Time to get movin', cowboy,' he said.

Bucko rose, running his fingers through his tousled hair. Dawn was breaking. The sky was a pearly-grey, gradually lightening even as the cowboy watched, and shot with streaks of mauve and crimson. He turned his attention to more material things. He took the coffee and buffalo-meat that was handed to him. After getting that under his belt he felt a whole lot better.

Cody and another man had climbed up ahead to do some scouting. They returned.

'All right, boys,' said the buffalo-leader. 'Let's get moving. We can't take the wagon up into the hills with us, so get as much ammunition as you can carry an' a rifle apiece. It'll be pretty well hidden here unless somebody comes right on to it.'

A few minutes later he was leading the silent band on their first steps into the vastnesses that lay ahead and above. They started to climb and they continued to climb, the going getting harder all the time until in parts they had to dismount and lead their trembling, sliding horses.

Bucko's nearest neighbour most of the time was a buffalo-hunter known as Billy Longhair because his thick, perfectly straight black hair reached well below his shoulders. He was a half-breed with not a little Pawnee Indian blood in his veins. His face had the high-cheeked inscrutable look that characterized his red brethren, the famous Pawnee scouts who were such a valuable ally of the white men. Longhair was no slouch as a scout himself and his black hawklike eyes were the first to spot the smoke signals. He even hazarded a guess at the identity of the red men who were sending the messages across country.

'Sioux,' he grunted.

The party halted and to a man followed with their eyes the direction of his lean pointing finger.

The graduated puffs of smoke engineered by some blanket-flapping redskin standing over a slow fire were rising from the hills about two miles to the right of them.

'Can you read anythin', Longhair?' said Cody.

'Nope,' said the scout. 'But I still figure it's Sioux.'

'Think they've spotted us an' are passing the word?'

The other shrugged. 'Maybe. An' then maybe not.' Judging by his demeanour he didn't give a hoot in hell either way. Danger was his middle moniker.

Cody stood in his stirrups and gazed all around.

'Don't seem to be anybody answerin' anyway,' he said.

'Don't hafta be,' said Longhair. 'Probably nothin' to do with us at all anyway.'

'We'll keep movin',' said the Leader. 'Keep your eyes peeled, boys.' The last sentence was totally unnecessary. Scenting danger and action the boys were wishing they'd got three pairs of eyes.

Longhair it was again who a little later made them look to their guns once more.

'More smoke,' he said. 'Looks like a camp-fire or some-thin' this time.'

Bucko's heart jumped within him as he too spotted the blue trickle of smoke half a mile maybe in front. Was this, so soon, the end of his quest? Was Lady Luck dealing him a good hand for a change?

'Let's get down, boys,' said Cody. 'Lead the horses.' He suited his action to the words.

They all dismounted and advanced more slowly.

'Looks like a fire all right,' said the Buffalo-leader softly.

'There's a faint trail here, Bill,' said Longhair.

'Shore is. Easy does it, boys!' Hardly were the words out of Cody's mouth when he clutched his shoulder. The wicked echoes of a rifle shot bounded and rebounded down the craggy slopes.

'Spotted, by heck!' boomed Dragon as the buffalo-hunters split-up, seeking cover.

Another shot took Bucko's hat off. He grabbed it. Judging by the neat round hole in his crown he had nearly been creased again. The sharp eyes of Longhair had spotted the marksman, and the little half-breed was triggering rapidly, sending a hail of lead up to the other's eyrie.

Cody had been slightly creased in the shoulder. Seated in cover with his back against a rock he staunched the slight flow of blood with a bandanna. Cowed by Longhair's wild but dangerous shooting the sniper dodged back into cover. In doing so he lost his advantage, for in those few split seconds the buffalo-hunters, and their mounts, vanished from sight. When the marksman peeked again a snapshot took his hat off.

Cody made a motion to Bucko. They split up, working in different directions. The cowboy wriggled on his stomach until he came to a gap. Then he rose on all fours and made a break for it. The rifleman opened up and a slug kicked up the dust at Bucko's heels. Then he was in cover once more. He began to wriggle away in the other direction, figuring to make a wide half-circle and come up behind the man. If Cody didn't get there first.

Suddenly there was a crackle of firing from up ahead. Bullets whistled around the buffalo-hunters, ricocheted wickedly from the rocks, awaking fiendish echoes. Evidently the sniper had suddenly gotten company. Bucko figured maybe they had tumbled on to one of Death Ordey's hideouts. He stopped crawling and rifle ready, peeked around the boulder that covered him. A slug almost took his nose off.

He waited, then tried again. This time no shots came his way. He saw a red-shirted shoulder. He sighted his rifle and squeezed the trigger. The shoulder disappeared. Above the rattle of gunfire he thought he heard a yell. He grinned. It felt good to be in action once more.

Bucko began to climb. The firing was spasmodic, little by little the buffalo-hunters were moving forwards. Bucko clambered round a huge boulder, and came suddenly in full view of the enemy. One of them saw him and with a hoarse shout of warning, raised his rifle. Bucko fired from the hip. The man screamed horribly, clutching at his middle.

The cowboy threw himself into cover as others opened up at him. He was unhurt and his heart sang with savage jubilation for, in that split second before he hid himself he had seen a skull-like face grinning at him. He had found Death Ordey!

However, if he didn't watch himself he figured he would never have a chance to get back at the skeleton-like killer. He was in a perilous position. He kept his head down and began to wriggle back a little. Furious firing broke out afresh. Bucko heard voices whooping and shrieking. That was his pards all right. He perched his hat on his rifle barrel and stuck it up above the rocks. No shots came his way.

He drew his colt and bobbed up. Up on a bluff directly opposite him he saw Cody and Longhair. They were blazing away and the bandits were turning and running. They knew this territory, they were vanishing like gophers into their holes. Bucko saw the beanpole form of Death Ordey and fired. He cursed. He had missed and now the bandit leader had dodged out of sight.

Bucko broke cover and bounded forward. Cody called to him; he paused. The buffalo-leader was shaking his head and pointing back. His words were wafted across.

'No good following on foot. Get horses.'

Almost reluctantly Bucko turned. But he could see the wisdom of Cody's plan. To plunge on foot after the bandits in their own country might mean being drygulched and finished without a chance.

He got back and forked his mount. All the buffalo-hunters were ready to ride. The only casualties were Cody's slight wound, which didn't bother him now, and a flesh wound in the thigh that one of the others had sustained. He had it bound tightly with a kerchief and was sitting his horse as gamely as ever, vowing he'd have a couple of scalps in return for the slight inconveniences the crease caused him.

They found the trail and rode as hard as the dangerous terrain would permit. Finally they broke into the open and looked down into the small valley from whence the smoke had drifted. There were two large log-cabins down there. Horsemen milled around them and, as the buffalo-hunters were sighted, they galloped away in the opposite direction and disappeared in twos and threes through a gap in the crags at the opposite side of the dip.

'So the skunks ain't gonna stop an' fight,' said one tobacco-chewing hunter.

'Death's too smart for that,' said Cody. 'He ain't gonna risk losing any more men. They've probably got dozens of hidey-holes in these hills. Still, it looks to me like we found one of their main ones anyway.'

He urged his horse gently down the slope. The others followed. They reached the cabins and the men dismounted and split up. If they couldn't have scalps at least they'd try to secure other spoils of the chase.

They found plenty of grub. Biscuits, bully-beef, beans, all the usual, as well as a few tins of luscious tongue. Plenty of coffee and a saucepan with boiling-water perched atop a redhot pot-bellied stove. The bandits had evidently been surprised preparing a meal. The hunters had it in their stead and it was good.

At length Cody said: 'I don't know what you boys think about it, but I think its pretty useless trying to follow Ordey right now. He's been warned an' he's no simpleton. He'll be waitin' for us next time, probably when we least expect him. I vote we go back to our wagon, hang on, then start all over again. He may think we've given up the chase altogether an' get careless. From here we can pick up the trail anytime we want. We'll come back and search the cabins later, when we've more time – besides, they might be occupied then!'

'That sounds like a good idea to me, Bill,' said Longhair. Most of the men figured the same.

'We might as well make use of this grub,' said Cody. 'Pack as much as you can.'

The boys set to work jubilantly, squabbling good-naturedly over those delicacies, the tinned tongue and the sweeter brand of biscuits.

'Maybe we ought to have a bonfire,' said one of the men. 'Make sure them yellow critturs don't come back here.'

But the general opinion was against this step, as being too dangerous on account of Indians. So apart from superficial damage, the outcome of unbridled strength and high spirits, the log cabins were left intact.

The buffalo-men rode out of the valley, past the little creek that was so convenient for the bandits, and back into the craggy slopes of the hills.

It was night when they reached the site of their camping ground where the foothills met the infinite plains. There a shock awaited them.

The wagon was in ruins; the canvas ripped to shreds, the woodwork smashed to fragments. Even the heavy iron-rimmed wheels had been torn apart. Most of the utensils and bedding had either disappeared altogether or been made useless and strewn about.

The same word burst from more than one pair of lips. '*Injuns.*'

The hoofprints of their frisky, unshod mustangs could be plainly seen in the soil all around.

'Well, there's nothing we can do here now, boys,' said Cody. 'We'd better hunt up another spot for a bivouac right away. This one's too dangerous.'

'You're sayin' some, Will,' said one of the men. 'The pesky red critturs may be watchin' us right now.'

'Quite likely,' said Cody. 'We jest gotta ride along as if nothing's happened. Their devils minds work in a queer way. They might decide to let us be.'

Longhair was a little way ahead; he had dismounted from his horse and was moving along on all fours like some peculiar species of bear.

'They've gone back up into the hills,' he said. 'The tracks end on these rocks here. They may be miles away now. There was about a dozen of 'em I guess, probably a bunch of young bucks havin' fun.'

'I hope that's all it was,' said Cody. 'Instead of a war-party, out after scalps – paleface ones in partic'ler.'

After half an hour or so of steady silent jog trotting they found another camping place in the shadows of a tower-ing over-hanging bluff. It was characteristic of them that not one suggested making tracks to Julesburg. With what scraps of bedding and blankets they had been able to salvage from the wreck of the prairie-schooner and with the slickers and small blanket-rolls most of them carried at their saddle-horns they made beds all around the base of the rocks.

'Keep well in, boys,' said Cody. 'Then nobody can roll anything over on us from above.'

Bucko found himself a spot between the leader and the

huge bulk of Dragon. The cowboy was lucky, or rather, provident, as he always carried a bedroll with him. Many times had he needed it while night-riding and tending sick dogies on the Texas ranges.

Like most of the men he leaned up against the rock for a while and smoked. A bottle of liquor, discovered in Death Ordey's hideout, was handed to him. He took a swig and passed it on. He smoked thoughtfully and looked around him.

It was dark and moonless, identical to last night. The sort of night his neighbour, Dragon, cursed. The stars were mere pinpoints dotted in a murky infinitude. The breeze from the plains was slow and sultry. Visibility was not very good but Bucko noted there was plenty of cover, in the shape of boulders, and craggy outcrops of rock close by. The horses were tethered in shelter there.

Cody dropped his glowing cigarette stub and crushed it beneath his boot-heel. He said:

'We'll take it in turns to watch. Four at a time. Two from that end, two from this.'

At both ends of the line of squatting shapes two men rose.

'All right, Bill,' they said.

'When you've done a couple of hours, wake your two neighbours each end . . . an' so on along the line.'

'All right.' The four men stole off a little way into the darkness. They were as noiseless as Indians. They had to be. The night swallowed all sight and sound of them. Far away a coyote yelped. Back in the hills another one answered with a long drawn-out howl that echoed and then faded.

Dragon spat into the darkness then, grunting and rolling like a grizzly-bear, composed himself for sleep. Cody got down too.

'Better get some shut-eye, Bucko,' he said. Then ominously: 'You might need all your strength.'

The cowboy ground his cigarette-end into the hard rock with his thumb.

'Shore,' he said and slid down beneath his blankets.

But for a time he did not sleep. His mind was too full of this new life he was facing, this destiny he had to get to grips with, those vows he had made. He heard the four guards return and awaken their neighbours. They in their turn stole off into the darkness.

So all was clear so far. Bucko dropped suddenly into heavy dreamless slumber.

A steel-like grip on his shoulder awakened him. There was a sound of gunshots, sibilant cries of 'Injuns.' Bucko rose between Cody and Dragon, his Colt in his hand. The three of them leapt to their feet almost simultaneously. Men were rising all along the line and darting into the darkness, peering over the barricade of rocks and rubble.

A horrible scream rang out. More shots. Another cry, guttural this time. Then a pandemonium of shots. A running man loomed up out of the darkness, paused as if tramfixed then with an awful bubbling cry fell forward on his face.

'Painter,' said Cody and bent over the fallen man.

Dragon and Bucko bounded forward; the whole band was moving forward. They joined up suddenly with the three other guards, Painter's comrades. One of them was cursing madly with a wounded arm.

'Injuns,' he said. 'They was on us before we spotted 'em. When we started shooting they ran for it.'

But they had not fled empty-handed. Painter had been scalped. He had also been slashed terribly all over with a tomahawk. He died in Cody's arms.

The whole band of tense, wide-eyed men crouched in cover until dawn. Eternal vigilance was their best weapon against the creeping red devils whose prime element was surprise.

SIX

Another dawn turned the hills to pearl and crimson as they buried Painter in a shallow grave beneath rocks where the buzzards and coyotes could not get at him. And they turned from the solemn task to meet another onslaught, this time of mounted savages, a big war-party in paint and full regalia sweeping across the plain towards them like a horde of screeching demons.

'They didn't lose a lot o' time in gettin' reinforcements to come an' wipe us out,' said Cody grimly. 'Keep low, boys, don't shoot till you see their eye-teeth.'

The hunters were almost jubilant as they sought cover. This was better than stealthy stabbing and slashing in the dark, this was the kind of fighting they welcomed. Although they were outnumbered at least two to one they were resolved to teach the pesky critters a lesson. Surely in broad daylight one white man should be a match for any two of the stinking red heathens.

'Most of 'em are Sioux;' said Longhair, and the assembled company knew they had a fight on their hands. The Sioux warriors were the finest fighting savages on the plains.

They were led by three chiefs in full regalia; wide headdresses containing eagles feathers; strings of beads; their bodies and faces painted in every conceivable colour and pattern. They each carried a long war-lance and scalps dangled from their belts.

'Look. The big one,' yelled Longhair. 'If that ain't Yellow Hand I'm a Chinaman's uncle.'

'It's Yellow Hand shore 'nough.' said Dragon. 'I can't mistake him. I nearly got his scalp once.'

'Well, here's your chance to try again, big boy,' yelled another of the men.

Bucko took a good look at Yellow Hand, he was by far the most imposing savage of the whole bunch. He was almost is big as the mountainous Dragon and the muscles rippled hugely beneath his glossy painted skin. Bucko had no more chance to weigh him up because, like the rest, he was squeezing trigger and pumping lead at the oncoming mob. One moment the chief was erect in the saddle, the next he had disappeared. But he had not been knocked from his horse, he had merely fallen back on the old Indian trick of swinging down and lying against the beast's flank.

The hunters' first volley had taken toll of the attackers. Painted forms lay still in the grass or wriggled painfully away. Still uttering their shrill insistent cries the others wheeled away, then, spreading out, came on again.

'By cracky!' yelled one hunter. 'They've got guns.'

It was seen by all that the majority of the redskins had rifles, some of them even the new Winchester repeaters. They fired from the saddle or, emulating Yellow Hand's example, clinging to their horses' flanks and shooting from their bellies.

'Good job fer us most o' the coyotes haven't learned to shoot straight yet,' said Cody drily.

Then he was silent as one buffalo-man sprang to his feet with a cry of agony and, cursing piteously, fell forward on his face. One wild shot had found its mark anyway.

Dragon spat a stream of tobacco-juice and squeezed

trigger once more. 'Four,' he counted. Then he said: 'It's a marvel to me how they manage to shoot at all from the positions they get into on them mustangs.' Then he gave a wild yell. 'Back, you red coyotes. Back!'

The oncoming line was waving and breaking once more. Three zealous young bucks reached the barricade. One had a Colt discharged full in his face and, spewing blood in all directions, toppled from the saddle. His wild mustang blundered on over the rocks and came to rest panting among the horses of the hunters.

The two other braves had flung themselves from their horses and were wrestling with their hated paleface foes. They didn't have much chance. One was killed by a crushing blow from the butt of a rifle; the other went down, with a revolver bullet in his throat, still clutching at the legs of the man who had shot him. The hunter beat at him with the butt of the gun, punctuating each blow with a blistering oath, until with a final gurgle the savage let go and lay still.

The attackers were not bothering to reform and charge now but were riding in madly, in ragged lines, many of them literally throwing their lives away in their eagerness for paleface scalps.

'They act as if they're either drunk or plumb crazy,' said one hunter.

Cody said: 'I'm damn glad we've got these rocks behind us so they can't come all around. Some of 'em are getting the range with them rifles. If they were circling us we'd be sittin' ducks.'

Bucko Martin marvelled at the way these men bawled chit-chat at each other in the midst of battle. He'd seen some fighting in his young life but there was something about these wild, fluttering red devils and their weird unceasing cries that made his flesh creep. He had no time to spit or talk, only to draw bead on fast-moving horsemen, squeeze trigger and whoop if he made a hit.

'They don't like this,' he heard Longhair yell. 'They're aimin' to get at close quarters.'

'Let 'em!' boomed Dragon. 'I'll get me a passel of scalps.' His wild harsh laughter echoed above the gunfire and the screeching. With the bushy black hair that hid his face, his eyes glaring from the midst of it, his mouth open and bawling cries to put the savages' yells to shame, he looked like some mad black demon.

The attackers came on with increasing speed and fury as if possessed by a collective craziness. Each one that went down seemed to be replaced immediately by two more. At some points along the line hand-to-hand fighting was already in progress; the hunters welcomed it and in battle many of them were almost as primitive as their opponents. They met the savages' shrieks with raucous war cries of their own, their tomahawks and lances with rifles and revolvers swung like clubs, with bowie-knives, fists, boots and claws.

Redskins flung themselves from their mounts in increasing numbers and tangled with the hated foe with demoniacal eagerness. It was not only their hate, their lust to kill, their thirst for scalps that drove them on – for many of the hunters smelled the fumes of cheap rot-gut whiskey on the hot breath of their assailants. Many of the red men tumbled over each other in their drunken haste and were systematically slaughtered by the shouting exultant pale-faces. But the latter were outnumbered. They had a grim fight on their hands.

Longhair cried out in agony as a tomahawk bit into the fleshy part of his arm. Then he dodged the next mad slash and, diving under the redskin's arm, drove his bowie-knife to the hilt in a muscular stomach. The savage screeched. Ignoring his own wound Longhair pushed the redskin backwards into one of his mates. The bloodstained knife remained in the half-breed hunter's grip. With one lusty stroke he cut the second savage's throat from ear to ear before he could rise.

He backed away behind the line and tore his shirt sleeve clean from the shoulder. He wrapped this tightly round the wound and tied it with his teeth and his good right hand. Then he looked around for further victims.

He saw a tomahawk flash and bury itself in the skull of one of his comrades.

Longhair uttered a terrible oath and sprang forward, his knife upraised. In close fighting this was his favourite weapon.

Chief among many of the others who, in hand-to-hand combat, favoured the trusty bowie was Dragon. His weapon was a giant among knives, a cross between a meat-cleaver and a bayonet and, in the hands of this blood-thirsty paleface, twice as dangerous as either of them.

Never had the redmen seen such black, glossy curly hair. Never such a scalp. Two of them sprang at him at once. He kicked one beneath the chin almost lifting his head from his shoulders. He shuffled like a bear, meeting the other's onslaught with a muscle-bound shoulder. The glittering tomahawk whistled harmlessly by. The redskin screamed in surprise and agony. He had been neatly disembowelled with one circular sweep of the huge knife.

Dragon backed away from the writhing form trying to cram its entrails back into its stomach with both hands, and winced as a thrust lance took a chunk of flesh from his shoulder. Its wielder was a head-dressed sub-chief but not, Dragon was disappointed to note, Yellow Hand. He bellowed and sprang at the savage's throat. Locked in combat, they swayed for a moment. But the brave was like a toy in the huge man's hands. The knife dipped and flashed, the savage cried out like- a tortured animal. Dragon's left hand came away holding the dripping scalp which, with another swift movement, he hooked to his belt. He lifted the squirming, crying body high above his head and threw it violently into the midst of the yelling red mob.

He saw the cowboy, Bucko Martin, grappling with another hideously-painted brave. But the younker did not need any help, he had his hands on the savage's throat and was squeezing the life from him. The writhing red body became limp. Bucko thrust it away from him and sprang immediately at another redskin who, with scalp knife ready was bending over a fallen, though still living, buffalo-hunter. He swung the heavy Colt in his hand and brought it down with all his strength on the feather-bedecked black head. The redskin crumpled without a sound. Bucko rolled the body away from the wounded man, an oldster who was almost singeing his own grey whiskers with the heat of his curses.

Bucko gripped the old man beneath his armpits and dragged him up to the rock-face.

The oldster, 'the Jackal' Bucko had heard him called, said plaintively: 'It ain't much, son, but it's in my laig. I can't stand. Of all the doggoned, dadblasted things to happen. . . .'

'Take it easy,' said Bucko. He found the wound.

'Tomahawk,' said the Jackal. 'Pesky crittur must've bin tryin' to chop off my legs an' call me Shorty.' He cackled shrilly.

The blade had dug deeply into the flesh at the side of the calf and smashed the bone. Bucko tied the leg up swiftly with the bandanna the oldster handed him.

'You've got your gun,' he said.

'Yeh. I blowed that red devil's brains out with it.' The old man hefted the heavy Frontier model Colt in his gnarled paw.

Bucko turned. The fighting was moving nearer.

'Look out, son,' screeched the Jackal suddenly.

He swung his gun and fired. The young buck who had been creeping up on them went over backwards. Then he rolled, almost to Bucko's feet. Most of his face had been taken away by the heavy slugs. Despite himself the cowboy shuddered. His blood had cooled a bit whilst he did his little task of mercy.

A thrown tomahawk which narrowly missed him and embedded itself in the old Jackal's chest made him see red again. The old man cried out once and became still, his grey beard slumped on his bloody breast.

Bucko clashed with the screeching brave, who had now drawn his scalping knife. The cowboy gripped the sinewy wrist, sweat bedewed his forehead as he forced it up and away. With his other hand the brave sought for the white man's throat. His hideous bedaubed face glared into Bucko's. The cowboy caught the full-blast of hot whiskey-stinking breath. He brought up his knee sharply into the savage's groin. The man gave a guttural grunt, his grip slackened. But he suddenly swerved his lithe oily body, throwing Bucko away from him. The cowboy lost his balance and fell on his back.

He saw the shining painted body hurtling towards him as the eager scalp-hunter sprang. He rolled desperately aside, the stabbing knife missed his face by a hair-breadth. Bucko rose to a sitting position, his gun in his hand. As the brave rose on his haunches he shot him in the side of the head. He rose, spinning the cylinder of the Colt with nervous fingers, cramming in fresh shells.

In the midst of the tossing mass of fighting men before him he suddenly espied Cody, hatless, his long hair flowing. He saw Yellow Hand, the Indian Chief, advancing on the buffalo-man. He saw their savage meeting. Then he suddenly had his hands full himself with a tomahawk-swinging buck.

Cody swayed to one side and Yellow Hand's plunging knife

tore a jagged hole in the sleeve of his coat. He slashed out with his gun at the broad, leering flat-nosed face. The sight drew a groove down the savage's painted cheek. Yellow Hand shrieked, more in rage than agony. He stabbed once more at this tall paleface who moved like quicksilver. He grunted with satisfaction as the sharp blade grated on the knuckles of the other's gunhand and the Colt fell to the dust.

Disregarding the hand, which, though bleeding freely, was not useless, Cody closed with the redskin, driving him back suddenly with crushing blows of his fist. For some strange reason most Indians are averse to fist-fighting. Yellow Hand was no exception. He staggered away from those stinging blows which sickened and surprised him. His knife weaved gleaming patterns in the air in front of him as he strove to pin this dancing white man.

He growled deep in his throat and threw himself forward. Cody's hard boot came up and kicked him in the stomach. But the Indian's middle was as ribbed and hard as a washboard. He took the kick in his stride and carried the buffalo-man with him. Locked in each other's arms they swayed for a moment then crashed to the ground.

Yellow Hand was on top, his fingers feeling for the redskin's favourite grip, at the throat, while he strove to break the hold of steel fingers that impeded the downward thrust of his knife-hand. What beautiful scalp-locks this pale-face had! So glossy, so long, so wavy. The big chief lusted after them like a spoilt child for candy and it maddened him that their possessor was so reluctant to part with them.

Cody tore with his bleeding hand at the fingers that clasped his throat. He wriggled his body and strove upwards with his knees. The sweat stood out in large beads on his forehead. His eyes glared into the mad eyes above, fetid breath sickened and enraged him. He spat into the lowering painted face.

Yellow Hand was so taken aback by this sudden new move by the crazy paleface that he started back and his grip slackened. It was the first time Cody had shocked a ruthless savage by spitting in his eye; he followed the spittle with his fist, bringing searing pain to that wounded member but having the satisfaction of feeling Yellow Hand wilt. He twisted and wrenched at the muscular red arm that held the knife; the steel flashed in a glittering arc and tinkled to the dust a few yards away.

'Now you red bastard,' said Bill Cody and he beat at the surprised red face above him. Yellow Hand was propelled from on top of him. He rolled, reaching for his scalp-knife in the dust. Cody lashed out with his feet. The redskin grunted with pain as a heavy nailed boot almost broke his arm. He forgot the knife and launched himself madly at his tormentor.

Cody rolled aside. The chief's heavy body missed him entirely. Cody was on his knees when Yellow Hand attacked again. For all his bulk the red man was fast. His arms wound round the buffalo-hunter's buckskin clad form and tightened. Cody had only one hand free; he balled it into a fist and wielded it like a hammer, striking terrific blows that seemed to explode in the other's face where the blood mingled with the paint and made an awesome picture. But Yellow Hand merely shook his head from side to side, mouthing with battered lips. He was mad with blood lust; he snarled and gnashed his teeth, trying to bite the white man's face. His arms tightened, he tried to bend Cody's body backwards.

The buffalo-man's face began to pale, although sweat ran from it in rivulets. The strain was terrible, his ribs seemed as if they would crack, his spine seemed to bend, he gasped for breath. His breath came in painful gusts as he beat once more at the mad man who held him. Yellow Hand's head was jerked back by the force of the blows, his grip slackened . . . but tightened again.

Cody changed his tactics suddenly. He pressed his fore-arm beneath the Indian's chin, against his throat. His teeth were bared, his eyes started from his head as he pressed harder and harder. Yellow Hand's broad, broken-nosed visage began to show the strain too. Thigh to thigh they strained, the white man and the red on a primitive level now, bloodlusting savages fighting for life.

Yellow Hand's tongue began to show between his teeth, his dark eyes glared and rolled, showing the whites horribly. He began to gurgle deep in his throat as the steel-like fore-arm pressed with increasing violence on his windpipe. But yet he would not unlock his arms from around the other's body. Perhaps his mind did not work that way. Perhaps he would rather be throttled to death. Cody was mighty afraid that if the mad savage did not let go soon they would both be goners. The pain in his chest and back was terrible and he could not breathe. He continued to exert his pressure mechanically, trying to force the redskin away from him and choke him at the same time. But all the time he was being pulled himself, crushed against the savage's broad hard chest, the pungent smell of the man and his paint like a living thing in his nostrils.

Yellow Hand was gradually being forced up from his knees. He was almost on his feet now, still binding Cody to him with arms that felt to the hunter like red-hot steel bands.

The savage was poised on his toes, all his weight against the white man, his head forced right back, glaring at the sky, when Cody suddenly let go. Caught off-balance, Yellow Hand lurched forward, his arms slackened. With fists, feet and knees Cody widened the breach. The redskin grunted at the punishment, strove to right himself, to tighten his grips once more . . . The buffalo-hunter hit him a terrible chopping blow across the adam's apple and taken utterly by surprise Yellow Hand found that his hands had been torn free, were clawing at nothing. No sound came from his bruised throat as he went over backwards. He fell beside his own scalping-knife. At the same instant the buffalo-man sprang for the weapon.

Both clawing hands, the red and the white, missed the weapon. Cody bit the dust but sprang to his feet immediately. He faced Yellow Hand as the towering savage rose.

The chief was an intelligent Indian, his madness had subsided, he knew now that only cunning could vanquish this paleface. More than ever he was determined to secure that glossy brown scalp.

The fighting had moved a little away from them but suddenly a lean, lusty young buck detached himself from the mêlée and advanced on Cody. Yellow Hand turned his head, snarling. This paleface was his, his alone. Those glossy tresses would not dangle at anyone else's belt. The buck turned away and next moment had his hands full with a stocky buffalo-hunter who seemed bent on throttling him.

Cody cleared the space between him and his opponent with one bound and struck the chief a surprise blow at the side of his head. Yellow Hand staggered, snarled in bewildered rage. He righted himself and reached for the other's throat. Cody dodged, circling. Yellow Hand circled with him, his hands held out like claws. Cody sprang again. This time the redskin dodged – he had wrestled and beaten all-comers when he was winning his place in the tribe as a young brave. Cody sprawled on his knees.

With that lightning twist of his body, he was on his feet again. He saw Yellow Hand bending for the knife. He kicked him on the side of the head. The Indian was bowled over. Cody sprang, retrieved the knife himself. Then he leapt on top of his fallen assailant. The red man was as tough as rawhide: he rolled clear. Both men half-rose together. Yellow Hand swooped, clawed hands reaching. Cody ducked low, stabbing with the knife; once, twice. The second time it was buried to the hilt in soft flesh. Warm blood gushed over the hunter's fist. The red chief gave a gurgling cry. His body went limp. His teeth were bared. His eyes glared; as Cody looked into them they glazed over. He twisted the knife free and let the body slump to the ground. He bent and tore the head-dress from the oily black head.

He stood erect, bloodstained knife held in one hand, the feathered head-dress waved aloft in the other, His voice rang out above the screeching and the babble.

'Yellow Hand is dead!' he cried. 'Yellow Hand is dead!'

Red faces and white turned towards him as he stood there, his eyes blazing, his nostrils distended, his long hair blowing around his shoulders. There was a lull in the fighting.

'Yellow Hand is dead!' yelled Cody again then with a wild whoop, swinging the head-dress around his head, the knife flashing in his other hand, he flung himself once more into the fray. The superstitious Indians, demoralized by the sudden death of their all-powerful chief and by the sacrilegious and crazy behaviour of this tall screeching paleface, turned and ran. Exultant yelling hunters pursued them for a little way. They brought a few more down with quick snap-shots and then let the remainder go.

Dragon stood over the body of Yellow Hand and said: 'Aw, Will, you knew I wanted his scalp.'

'Have it then,' said Cody. 'I don't want it.'

The huge, hairy man looked disgusted. 'You know I can't take his scalp unless I killed him myself, yer long-legged sonofagun.'

'Pity,' said Cody. 'He's got such a lovely head of hair.'

SEVEN

Old Judge Mackey and Ralph Burndon were in the tent when Cody and Bucko Martin entered.

Tall, blond Burndon rose to his feet and shook hands with both of them.

'Mighty glad to see you both back all in one piece,' he said. 'I hear you had some trouble.'

'Five men killed, three wounded,' said Cody soberly. 'The wounded are out of danger.'

'Give thanks for small mercies,' said Burndon.

'The General back?' asked Cody.

'No, not yet. We're expecting him any day now.'

'Anythin' come in across the wire?'

'No,' said Burndon. 'And you? Did you find out anything?'

'We found out the Injuns are getting plenty supplies of rifles and rotgut liquor from somewhere. We caught up with Ordey but he got away. He knows every inch of the hills. We finished off a couple of his men.'

'He's scared then?'

'Maybe.'

'Was he mixed up with the Indians?'

'We don't know, they attacked us afterwards. Can't tell whether Ordey sicked 'em on to us or not. They'd been drinking whiskey before they came. They stank with it. Maybe Ordey filled 'em with it.'

'He's the one we've always suspected of peddling the whiskey this end. It's feasible he's handling the rifles as well.'

'Yeh, but how? He's mighty clever. He's probably got a go-between right here in town.'

'Where else? But to find him in this hell-hole is some task – when most of the bad men in the territory are in league with Ordey.'

While Burndon and Cody conversed Bucko sat opposite Mackey. Suddenly the old judge spoke in his querulous voice. 'So you've had your first taste of Injun fighting, young feller.'

'Yes, suh, quite a mouthful.'

'And you came thru' all right?'

'Narry a scratch.'

'Handy with a gun?'

'Kinda.'

As the old man shot these questions at the young Texan his little sharp eyes sparked from amid the wrinkles in the pinched parchment-like face. There was fire and irritable life in those eyes. And the light of an unquenchable will. Bucko began to take a liking to the old jackass.

Suddenly Mackey said: 'I came from the Panhandle myself – many years ago – a little town called Gopher.'

'I know it.'

'Do you?' For a moment the other's voice lost its querulous tone. His eyes sparked more vividly than ever. 'What's the ol' place like now, boy?'

'Purty much the same. Quiet. Growin' tho'.'

'It was too quiet for me,' said the old man. 'But it's better country than this. Here the redskins are better'n most of the whites.' He made the motion of spitting and his eyes flamed. 'Scum!'

Then he subsided, muttering to himself, the wrinkled lids shading his eyes now as he slumped hunch-backed in his chair.

Bucko heard Ralph Burndon say something that made him prick up his ears more.

'Bill Hickok's somewhere around, Will.'

'Bill Hickok? You sure?'

'Yes, I've seen him.'

'Well, what's he doin' in this neck o' the woods?'

'Looking for trouble as usual I suppose,' said Burndon drily.

Bucko had cause to be interested. Who in the West of that day had not heard of Wild Bill Hickok of Abilene?

'You know him don't you, Will?' said Burndon.

'Yeh, kinda.'

'Well, get hold of him. We don't want the other side to hire him. He's too dangerous a man for that. We want him on our side.'

'Where is he?'

'That's what I don't know. In one o' the gambling-hells I suppose if he's still in town. He said he'd only come in to look the place over.'

'Why didn't you fix something up?'

'I didn't get a chance. You know Hickok. He just spit at my feet and swaggered off.'

'If he throws his weight about in Julesburg among people who don't recognize him he'll soon be in a fight,' said Cody.

'Which might be just too bad for the other fellow,' said Burndon.

Bucko got the drift of that. Hickok was a real wild man when he was roused and he didn't care who got killed. If anybody could clean up Julesburg it was he. But would he want to? Or would he prefer to gamble and drink with the 'underworld' characters of 'Hell on Wheels.' He was a mighty unpredictable cuss. All this Bucko knew by hearsay. But he had yet to meet in the flesh the West's most notorious gunman.

Conversation flagged for a while. Then Cody said: 'Well, so we're no more forrarder in our investigations, Ralph?'

'It doesn't appear so. Whatever information Lemmings had he either carried in his head or it was taken from him when he was killed.'

Bucko figured Lemmings must have been the scalped trooper who had lived to speak that terrible day on the Platte. The thought of it, and what had happened after it, made his heart contract again.

'White devils' work,' said Cody. 'And who other but Death Ordey?' He turned abruptly on the cowboy. 'Let's get movin', Bucko. We may bump into Hickok.'

Burndon bade them an affable 'good-night.' Judge Mackey merely grunted.

Once outside Bucko asked Cody who and what Ralph Burndon was.

'He's a sort of an agent for the Government,' said Cody. 'Works as a go-between them an' the U.P. Easygoing cuss. I always get on well with him. Southerner originally I think. Deep South.'

'Yeh, his talk's got that flavour,' said Bucko. 'An' how about the judge? What's he do? – when he ain't half-asleep.'

Cody grinned. 'He's a sort of a legal adviser to General Casement and the railroad – about the only real lawyer in Julesburg I guess. Don't let the old man fool you, Bucko. He's a very active member of the team. He's got a place in town but he spends most of his time in that tent.'

The two men moved on down the street and entered one of the largest honky-tonks, a place called The Golden Tiger. It was pretty shabby, only the varied habiliments of the customers who jammed in its four walls made it at all colourful. There was plenty of dirty floor space, plenty of tables, but not enough seats to go round. Many men, and women – of one particular kind – jostled and jammed, treading on each other's toes, laughing, cursing, drinking, gambling. There were faro tables, superintended by hard-eyed gentry in black, where a man could 'buck the tiger,' there were a couple of roulette wheels – and hosts of independent games going strong. As usual the railroad workers outnumbered everybody else by two to one and there was a subtle air of unrest over the whole assemblage, a moaning, discontented undertone. The workers had not yet been paid and the general opinion was that this money had been in the wrecked train and the redskins and renegades had gotten away with it.

By now both Bucko and Cody knew this was not so, but when and how the money was to reach the end of the track they did not know – perhaps only General John Casement did and he was not in Julesburg ... anyway, at times like this – Cody opined – the redbearded old soldier was very cautious and inclined to keep his own counsel.

The two men were greeted from on all sides, even the workers had nothing against the Buff'ler; he at least didn't welsh on his meat-contract. And that the dark young man who looked like a cowboy was a partner of his was good enough for them.

It was Bucko who spotted Dragon first and, right away, he sensed there was something wrong. The huge man was over by the bar and was glaring murderously at some one in front of him whom the cowboy could not see. As he watched, Dragon moved forward with that peculiar, menacing bear-like gait of his.

Bucko grasped Cody's arm and swivelled him round.

'Bill, look! It 'pears like Dragon's on the prod.'

The buffalo-leader took one look then said, 'Come on,'

and began to elbow his way through the crowd. Other people were looking in that direction now and as the two men moved forward they heard Dragon's booming tones but could not hear what he said.

There was an ominous lull in the babble of sound, they heard a noise like the growl of a beast, the thud of a blow and the crash of falling, splintering furniture. Then they broke through the press with a final rush and spotted Dragon and his opponent.

Bucko took in the whole scene with one practised glance. A big red-haired squint-eyed man lay on the floor amid the wreckage of a broken chair and partly shielded by an upturned table. A gun glittered on the boards out of reach of his hand. Dragon was leaning across the table, his huge hairy hands out, reaching for his prey, who, blood now trickling from his lips, was cursing madly and trying to rise.

Cody started forward, the cowboy a little behind him. A hard-looking character against the bar, out of the line of Dragon's vision, suddenly drew a gun. Bucko Martin paused, straddle-legged and blurred in motion; his right hip was wreathed in smoke from which spurted a wicked tongue of flame as the gun boomed. With a cry of surprise and agony the gunman clutched at his smashed hand; his gun arched in the air and clattered to the boards. Bucko backed up beside the man and buffetted him on the back of the head sending him on his face, one foot hooked in the brass rail. Back against the bar, gun poised, Bucko stood watchful. His blood sang with the joy of action, this kind of a ruckus was meat and drink to him. Cody had gotten hold of Dragon's arm and, yelling in the blood-lusting monster's ear, was endeavouring to drag him away from the fallen man. Dragon shook him off with a deep snarl and turned savagely on his new tormentor.

'You big skunk,' gritted Cody. His voice seemed to

check the giant; he shook his head furiously from side to side like an irritated grizzly and the mad light went from his eyes.

'He was tryin' to take a rise out of us, Will,' he said. 'He got me mad. I forgot his damned gammy leg – he thought I wouldn't, I guess.'

The fallen man was helped to his feet and put on a chair. His left leg stuck stiffly out in front of him as he sat down. His face was suffused with crimson, his squint-eye blazed with rage, his ragged red hair seemed to stand on end. He said in a trembling voice: 'Thanks fer nothin', Cody. I guess you didn't want your favourite boy to bash a cripple man who couldn't defend himself.'

'Good job for you you have got a busted leg, Johnson,' said Cody, 'Otherwise I'd've let Dragon tear you in half while me an' my partner here took care of your pet gunmen.' He indicated with a sneer the groaning man on the floor and the other two hands who stood by Johnson and glowered impotently into the mouth of Buck's Colt.

'I won't allus have a busted leg, Cody,' snarled the other. 'It's getting better.'

'I'm glad to hear that,' said the tall man softly. 'And Dragon is I guess – hey, Dragon?'

The huge man, sober now, leered horribly. 'Sure thing, I'll tear it off for him when it's better.'

'When it is better and he can't use it for an excuse, he'll probably be too yellow to open his trap,' said the leader.

His face almost purple now with impotent fury, Johnson tried to rise then slumped back in his chair.

'I won't forget this,' he snarled.

'Neither will we,' Cody told him. 'Better pick your gun up an' next time you draw on one o' Bill Cody's men you'll have to try to be faster or the government 'ull have to send another meat-boy to make the team up. Dragon could've killed you – self-defence you know. You were lucky.'

One of Johnson's men picked the gun up and handed it to his boss. Bucko's keen blue eyes watched them, hawk-like, until the weapon was safely ensconsed in its holster.

Johnson had cooled down. His men righted the table and began to gather up the cards that were strewn across the floor. Two others picked up the wounded man and carried him through the crowd.

Cody and his two friends turned to go. As they did so, Longhair and three more buffalo-hunters joined them, wordlessly, making a sort of rear-guard as they marched from the Golden Tiger.

Johnson's mocking voice rang out. 'Cody's three-ring circus,' he jeered.

Although he was trying to be funny now and people laughed at his pronouncement he could not know that his jeering words carried a hint of prophecy.

Bucko and Cody left the other four at a gaming table in another hell and, after eats and a quiet smoke in the Palladin, went back to Mother Brannigan's. The old dame wasn't there, neither was the young clerk, but the half-breed, deaf-and-dumb slavey, Minnie, met them at the bottom of the stairs and muttered and gesticulated.

'What's eatin' her?' said Bucko.

'Couldn't say,' said Cody. 'She gets het-up over nothin' at all does Minnie. C'mon.'

They passed the girl and went on upstairs. Bucko looked back. She was standing on the bottom-step looking up at them with big, dark eyes. Despite the vacuousness of her dark face she was not unattractive. In fact, Bucko had to admit she was all woman. The tawdry pink dress she wore was clean and well-patched but too small for her. It was probably some dance-hall girl's cast-off and revealed a lot of Minnie's shapely limbs and soft brown flesh. The girl tried to say something else. It was a pitiful sound and

Bucko quickly turned away.

He heard her feet pattering away across the floor. Then the outer door banged. Suddenly other feet sounded upstairs, heavy dragging feet. A voice bawled: 'You bitch, I'll get yer!' Then followed a string of strangled curses. The feet thudded nearer.

Cody ran on to the landing, Bucko behind him. A man in shirt-sleeves was staggering towards them, his one arm limp and dripping with blood, his other hand brandishing a gun.

'Hold it, friend,' said Cody. He bounded forward and caught the man as he swayed. 'You're bleeding like a hamstrung hog,' he said.

Bucko ran to help. They half-carried the man through the open door of the room he had evidently just vacated and tipped him on the bed. All the time he struggled with them feebly and cursed to be let go so he could 'shoot that bitch'! Cody had to take the gun away from him.

They tipped him up on the bed and Cody drew his knife and slashed away the shirt sleeve.

'You've got a nasty cut, partner,' he said.

The other's wrath had subsided. He was weakly sullen. 'I'm lucky I ain't a goner,' he said. 'The treacherous bitch.'

'Been getting fresh with our Minnie have you, stranger?'

'I only grabbed her round the waist kind of playful like.'

'An' she knifed you,' said Cody. 'You ain't been in Julesburg long I guess or you'd've found out about Minnie. She hates most men – must've had a bad time with 'em when she was a kid I guess, her being deaf and dumb an' all. I guess you asked for it, friend.'

'Asked for it!' burst out the man. 'I hardly touched her.'

'Keep still,' said Cody. 'You're still bleeding badly.'

The man lay still as the buffalo-man tore a strip from the already blood-spattered sheet and wadded the wound with it.

Then the man said: 'I swear I'll get her when I get up

an' out.'

'I wouldn't do that if I were you, friend,' said Cody.

'No, suh,' echoed Bucko and glowered down at the wounded man. He didn't like the look of the greasy, puffy-faced cuss. The man dropped his eyes.

'You see, partner,' said Cody conversationally, 'You scared Minnie. She ran out into the street. She might tell some of the boys – if she can make 'em understand. She tried to tell us an' we were in too much of a hurry to bother. Anyway I should lay low for a bit. Some o' the boys might be lookin' for your scalp.'

'All right,' said the man and muttered a surly 'thanks' as the buffalo-hunter finished dressing the wound.

'Got business in Julesburg, friend?' said Cody.

'Yeh, I've come to work on the railroad.'

'Well, there ain't no real call to pay dues to Ma Brannigan you know. The railwaymen've got their own sleeping quarters.'

'I know,' said the man, almost vehemently. 'But I don't want to sleep with that scum.'

As they turned to go Cody flung a parting shot at the reclining man. 'At least most o' that scum, as you call them, wouldn't try to take the rise out of Minnie.'

At the door Bucko turned too, his blocky form braced a little, his hand on the butt of his gun. 'I should advise you to let the gel alone pardner,' he said.

The other man looked up, his white puffy face sullen, his eyes shielded by heavy lids. He did not speak.

When they got into the passage the cowboy said mockingly to his companion, 'You're quite a little horse-doctor ain't you, Mr Cody?'

The other man said: 'I was a medical-orderly for a bit when I was in the Army.'

'You been quite a few things in your young life ain't yuh?'

'Yes,' said the hunter. 'I like change.' He paused as they stood on the landing for a moment, then he said: 'I guess we'd better go and find Minnie an' tell her it's safe to come back here.'

They found the half-breed girl having a cup of coffee in the Palladin Eating House. With her was one of Cody's men, a hard-bitten cadaverous individual known as Beany, who rose on their arrival.

'Has somebody down at the house been getting fresh with Minnie?'

'Yes, but . . .'

The thin man blundered hotly on: 'Show me the yeller-livered coyote, I'll carve his guts out.'

'Take it easy, Beany, an' sit down,' said Cody.

The man glared at his leader but he plumped down in his seat again.

Cody said: 'This gink's a stranger. He didn't do much harm to the gel. He didn't have a chance to. Minnie's done a right fancy bit of carving on him.'

'Good fer you, gel,' said Beany, turning and grinning at the girl. She smiled back, understandingly, revealing small regular white teeth and, momentarily, her dark eyes lit up. At that time she looked savagely beautiful.

'Me an' Bucko patched the skunk up an' cooled him down,' said Cody. 'He'll leave Minnie alone in future.'

'He'd better,' said the cowboy darkly. He had taken a violent dislike to that white-faced galoot back at Mother Brannigan's. Maybe it was because he hated to see dumb things ill-used. He almost laughed out loud at this thought. In many senses Minnie was far from dumb. She was a little wild-cat. The cowboy was pretty sure she had tried to put paid to the man. She was half a savage, a deaf and dumb savage, and she acted like one.

Cody suddenly said: 'Wild Bill Hickok's in town, Beany. Have you seen him?'

The cadaverous man looked startled. 'That's news to me,' he said. 'An' I ain't seen him.'

'You'd know him if you did see him?'

'Yeh, I guess so. I seen him once before. He was a US Marshal at the time. He killed a couple of friends o' mine – caught 'em with stolen cattle. I guess they asked for it. They didn't have much chance with Hickok.'

Bucko and Cody rose. The latter beckoned to the girl. She followed them as they bade 'so-long' to Beany.

Cody turned again. 'If you see Hickok ask him to come an' ask for me down at Ma's place.' As they quitted the Palladin he carried on talking to Bucko. 'I don't expect he'll come in any case. He don't like bein' sent for. Still, it's unusual for him to lay low like this. Nobody seems to've seen him or even heard that he's in town. Maybe he jest rode thru' an' is on the trail again now.'

They entered the rooming-house to discover that Ma had got back. Minnie ran to her with gesticulations and mouthings that only the old dame could understand. The huge fearsome-looking woman's hairy brow became black as thunder as she began to get the drift.

'I'll have that snake out pronto on his neck,' she said.

Half-way up the stairs Cody turned and said: 'Call us if you need any help, Ma.'

'Shore thing,' echoed Bucko.

'Hey, Bill,' called the woman. 'Come back down here. I've got somethin' mighty interesting to tell yer.'

The two men descended the stairs again. Ma said: 'Did yer know Wil' Bill Hickok was in town?'

'Yes, we've been looking for him. Have you seen him?'

'Have you seen him?' Ma leered. 'Y'know, Will – I knew him from way back!'

'Yeh.'

'Wal, when he found out I was in business in Julesburg he came lookin' for me. But he came to the wrong place.'

The old dame's grin widened.

Cody said: 'You mean he came to the other place?'

'Yeh,' chortled Ma. 'An' one o' the gels made a pass at him. He didn't like her so he shot two-three o' the lamps out and lit out o' the place.'

Cody began to laugh. 'I can just imagine him,' he said. 'Bill don't like bein' rushed. He likes to pick 'em for himself. Maybe – bein' surprised like – he didn't feel like it. Where did he go?'

'That's what I don't know,' said Ma. 'I ain't seen hide nor hair o' the big son-of-a-gun. I guess the gels scared him plumb outa the territory.'

'Well, we ain't gonna spend any more time lookin' for him,' said Cody. He turned to his companion. 'Come on Bucko, let me an' you have a nightcap in my room.'

As they drank their whiskey they heard Mother Brannigan stump up to their wounded neighbour's room. They heard the altercation that followed, Ma's booming tone drowning the vicious whining of the man's. There was a sound of bumping and hasty movements as the man got his things together. Then they heard the sounds of the landlady, still booming indignantly, shepherding him downstairs.

'That's the last we'll see of him in this place,' said Cody.

'An' we didn't even find out his name,' said Bucko in mock grief.

They talked desultorily. At length the conversation turned to the subject of the fracas in The Golden Tiger earlier that night. Bucko heard more about the other buffalo-leader, Cody's hated rival, Johnson. He remembered Mother Brannigan had told him a little about the situation.

'Bitter Creek they call him,' said Cody. ' 'Cos that's where he came from.' Such was the custom in this end-of-track 'Hell-on-Wheels' where men, good and bad, from all over the States, came to seek excitement and fortune. Many would not say where they came from, would not even give their names. It was impolite as well as dangerous to ask too many questions. These enigmas of human flotsam went by such appellations as 'Shorty,' 'Skinny,' 'Lofty,' 'Dutch,' 'Jock,' 'Curly,' 'Red,' 'Monk' or whatever name their appearance, colouring or particular idiosyncrasies suggested. If a man mentioned his hometown or place, or what he chose to call his home-town, he was labelled accordingly. Hence 'Bitter Creek' Johnson. Although Mack Johnson was, like Cody, a trusted employee of the US Army, coupled with the Union Pacific Railroad, with a contract to supply meat enough to feed everybody who was employed by the two allied juggernauts. And oft-times there was a bonus for the man whose hunters brought in the most. Little wonder there was rivalry between the two leaders, both wild and strongly-individualistic men. Probably Johnson, a cross-grained cuss himself, envied Cody his popularity in Julesburg, his friendship with General Casement and others. Maybe there were even deeper motives.

'Johnson's had some bad luck lately,' said Cody. 'His last meat-party was attacked by a big party of Injuns. A lot of his men were killed. Those who got away, Johnson among 'em, had to ride for it and left the wagons loaded with meat an' hides. Them redskins sure had a picnic. Johnson got wounded in the leg. He ain't a pleasant cuss at the best o' times. I guess that was the last straw. He must be boiling-up inside of him.'

'Wal, that's no reason to go takin' it out of you an' your boys,' said Bucko. 'You ain't done him no harm have you?'

'No, except maybe that my men usually bring in more stuff than his do.'

'I ain't surprised after seeing some of 'em,' said Bucko. 'They look to me more like professional gunnies than buffalo-hunters.'

'Yeh,' said Cody. 'He's got a lot of that kind hangin' around with him. Most o' them you saw were men he'd got to replace those that were killed in the raid.' He paused . . . 'A bunch of us took a chance and went out to look for the bodies an' the wagons. There was hardly a trace. The redskins had taken the lot – bodies an' all it seemed. They do that sometimes. Some o' the old-timers say they roast 'em an' eat 'em, but I gotta see that before I believe it. Johnson said all the men they left were dead but I figure some of 'em were only wounded. The red-devils 'ud have their sport with 'em.'

The Buffalo-leader's brow clouded. 'An' if that ain't bad enough, now white men are selling these savages whiskey an' guns – an' riding with 'em and leading them.'

Bucko thought this was a good chance to broach the suggestion he had running through his mind right then. 'Bill,' he said. 'Why don't we go out scoutin' after that Death Ordey an' his boys while the trail's still warm. Just me an' you or a few of us. We might do better than riding out in a bunch – particularly if Ordey's got spies in town, as no doubt he has. Slip away I mean an' don't tell anybody where we're goin'. What d'yuh think, Bill?'

'I think it's a good idea,' said Cody. 'I've been thinkin' of it myself. Just me, you, Dragon an' Longhair. They'd jump at it, both of 'em – particularly the big feller, all the time he's in town he's in trouble an' when he goes home I believe his squaw nags his ears off.'

Bucko grinned but when he spoke again he could not keep the eagerness out of his voice. 'Why don't we then?'

'You're a glutton for punishment ain't you?' said the other. Then his face sobered. 'In the circumstances I guess I'd be the same – if we catch up with Death he's all yours, Bucko.'

'It's a deal. We're goin' then.'

'I'd like to see General Casement first. He should be

here soon . . . An' when he does come back I hope to find he's done something about the U.P. payroll. It's well behind. The workers are mighty restive. The section-bosses won't be able to keep 'em in check much longer – even if they want to. I guess you can't blame any of 'em for kickin'. It's a good job the Injuns haven't bothered 'em for the last few days . . . Incidentally, our own money is with that payroll too. How are you britched, Bucko? I can . . .'

'I'm all right, thanks Bill,' said the cowboy. 'Money don't bother me none . . . I take it then we ride as soon as you've seen the General?'

'Yes. But I guess we won't wait too long for him.'

'Maybe in the meantime we oughta hunt up the mighty Mr Hickok an' ask him to come along,' said Bucko drily.

Cody grinned. 'I guess Wild Bill wouldn't fancy crawlin' around on his stomach in the dark. I guess he'd sooner do his fightin' under the bright lights where he can see the other fellow bat his eyes.' He suddenly rose. 'I guess I'll go right now to see if the General's back.'

Bucko hadn't been asked to come along so he did not follow. This abrupt secrecy of Cody's, this love of mystery, was one thing he did not like about the tall hunter. But he guessed maybe there was a reason for it. Maybe it had to be.

EIGHT

Dawn etched the foothills like crouching sentinels over the wild country. It washed gently over the ghost town of North Platte, as if loath to reveal fully its squalor and decay; it touched the sightless windows with pink fingers in warning that another bright day was near.

But the people of North Platte did not awake to greet the dawn, they were nearly all old or useless and they lay abed dreaming of past glories; of the time when North Platte was a rip-roaring end-of-track town like Julesburg. But those ribbons of steel had moved remorselessly on and, with them, the workers, the gamblers, the women, the noise, the lights, the wealth, the action and the laughter.

The spears of the dawn investigated the silent street and suddenly transfixed the sagging façade of the wreck of the Maple Leaf Hotel with its lopsided sign and broken windows. For the Maple Leaf despite its looks, was one of the few places that was still doing business. And, more surprising still, it was already showing signs of life. An old man came out on the front stoop (the wooden sidewalk had long since been broken up for firewood) and tossed a pailful of dirty suds across the cart-rutted street, laying the dust like treacle and disturbing a lizard that had been crawling there seeking the sun.

The old man looked around him with interest for a time, his toothless jaws champing at his quid. Then he peered into the bucket to make sure it was empty. Satisfied, he gave a final look around, spat a stream of baccy-juice after the suds, then turned and went back into the hotel.

In the dim dusty interior he put the bucket down on the floor and crossing to the uncarpeted stairs began to ascend. Once at the top he walked along the landing and rapped at the third door.

'Yeh?' said a deep voice. 'Who's there?'

'I can git some breakfast now if you want it, sah,' said the oldster.

'All right. Go ahead,' said the voice. 'I'll be right down.'

'Yes, sah,' The oldtimer shuffled off.

Inside the room the man clambered from beneath the single, patched sheet. He still wore his trousers and navy-blue and grey check shirt. His feet were clad in thick grey woollen socks. His red bandanna was draped over the head of the rusty iron bedstead with peeling patches of green paint. So was his thick serge grey vest with the red piping on the lapels. His battered greasy Stetson was perched on the pillar, with the brass knob missing, at the foot of the bed. Two chairs were drawn up with their backs to the bed and just under an armslength away from it. Slung over the back of one was a gunbelt, the holsters dangling, the twin gun-butts protruding so that as the man lay in bed all he had to do to reach a gun was snake out a hand. His high-boots with their scuffed rider's heels and fancy steel spurs were stood up-right in the middle of the floor. A queer place to put a pair of boots – but these, together with the two chairs, would have tripped-up any stealthy visitor who tried to creep into the room during the night. This man evidently had enemies . . . Or maybe he was just naturally cautious.

He rose and stretched. He was a big man, over six feet

and superbly built, his body tapering from wide shoulders and a deep chest to a flat, hard stomach and narrow hips. His thigh-muscles bulged through the tight cloth of his trousers as he reached. His face was handsome too, brown, strong, well-formed, the nose slightly hooked, the lips thin but pliable. His eyes were a clear blue, but inclined to coldness. His hair was brown and curled around his ears.

The first thing he did after flexing his healthy muscles was to reach his gun-belt and buckle it on. The twin Colts nestled on his thighs as if they were part of them. He raked the room with swift eyes. The closed door, the uncurtained window open at the top to let in a little air; the small rickety washstand with its pitcher and bowl, the towel and soap placed beside them; the worn mat on the bare boards of the floor, the boots and the two chairs. Still in stockinged feet he crossed to the window and looked out. The street was deserted, its dullness and squalor enlivened here and there by a dappled rosiness. Might be a nice day, might be a stormy one. The breeze was still.

He turned away and crossed the room again to the washstand. He peered into the pitcher then tilted it and poured a stream of water into the bowl. He opened his shirt collar wide at the neck and turned it down. He rolled up his sleeves to reveal muscular forearms. He reached for the soap and began to wash himself thoroughly.

He finished and wiped himself with the rough off-white towel. He ran his fingers a few times through his damp tousled hair. It fell into place on his well-shaped head in waves and little curls. He sat on a chair and pulled on his boots. He tied his bandanna losely around his throat and donned his vest, leaving it swinging open. He moved the two chairs away from the bed and then reached for his hat and clapped it nonchalantly on the back of his head. All his stuff was good, but well-worn.

Now he looked at peace with the world. He crossed to

the door. His hand was on the latch when he paused. His keen ears caught distant sounds. He went back to the window and looked out again, craning his neck. He could not see anything. The sound was just a dull throb against his eardrums. He shrugged. Maybe he was hearing things. He went across to the door again, opened it, passed through, and went downstairs.

The oldster greeted him with a toothless grin. 'Right in the back, sah,' he said. 'Everythin's ready.'

The big man crossed the dusty lobby, his firm steps awakening echoes, and for a moment it seemed to the old man that all the place's vanished greatness was back once more. He ushered his visitor across the hall. Through the open door of the kitchen came the smell of fried bacon.

'That's good,' said the big man. His voice, like his carriage and manner, was strong and resonant.

'We thought you wouldn't mind havin' it in the kitchen, sah,' said the oldster. 'Its warm an' comfortable in there.'

'Suits me, oldtimer,' said the man. He strode through the kitchen door. Then he paused. 'Good mornin', ma'am,' he said.

The white-haired old lady who was cutting bread at the table answered him in a reedy voice. 'Sit down, mister,' she said.

'Thanks.' The big man seated himself at the bare scrubbed board. With the air of a conjuror the old man whipped a large steaming plate of bacon, fried potatoes and string beans in front of him. The old lady silently passed him bread. He nodded in thanks and gave them both a thin-lipped smile. Then he set to with gusto.

He wiped up the plate in double-quick time and the old man offered him more. He soon rubbed that off too. Then, after taking a swig of the hot coffee the old lady had put before him he leaned back in his chair with a sigh and lit a cigarette.

'Mighty fine vittles you get here, my ol' friends,' he said. 'I'm kinda surprised.'

'We get 'em from the Crow Ranch,' said the old man. 'Pete Crow keeps a few hogs an' he's got his own vegetable patch.'

'Has he got much stock besides?'

'Yep, quite a lot of cattle.'

'Yep,' said the big man reflectively. 'I guess this is decent grazing-ground. Don't the Injuns bother him none?'

'Not for a long time. They followed the railroad. When the lines were bein' laid by Pete's land he useter be bothered with 'em – nearly got scalped once. The railroad men useter help him drive 'em off. But Pete didn't like the railroad – he lost a helluva lot of cattle through it, what with Injuns and stampedes an' suchlike. He says it'll be worse when the trains start comin' through in force. An' it's takin' his trade too, 'cos o' the stockyards they're openin' on the line further back. He says North Platte oughta be turned into a herd town . . . Maybe it will be.' The old man's voice was wistful.

'Yeh, maybe it will,' said the big man. 'You don't get much trade here as it is do you? . . . Still, I came here for a rest.'

'Nope. I don't get much trade,' said the old-timer. 'Saddletramps now an' then. Buffalo-men an' suchlike. But me an' Hattie are getting too old to be movin'. Maybe we'll see North Platte on its feet again before we die . .' He waxed philosophical: 'The railroad gave birth to it and the railroad killed it – leastways its dying. Maybe the railroad 'ull be the means of its rebirth.'

But the stranger did not seem to be listening to the babblings of the half-educated old man. He said: 'Sounds like you got more visitors, pop. Busy times lately, eh?'

'Eh? I don't know o' no more visitors. Unless my neighbours are havin' them. An' they're too idle to get up yet, I guess. 'Cept maybe Cal Buggins at the store.'

The big man had been right about the wagon-wheels, they were rumbling into North Platte now. But he seemed to have suddenly lost his curiosity. He sat indolently and smoked as the rumbling wheels came to a stop in the street outside. When the old man went out of the kitchen he did not follow him.

Above the shuffling steps of the old-timer boomed the sound of thudding bootheels on the bare board floor. A voice shouted 'Anybody home? Look alive!' Then: – 'Oh, hallo, pop. You'll hafta move faster than that – we want coffee an' eats pronto.'

The old man's trembling voice came clearly. 'You won't get nothin' ef you don't moderate your tune, young feller.'

The old lady said softly: 'Jake's mighty independent.'

The big man nodded; despite his indolent attitude he looked alert now, listening.

From in the hall came the sound of ribald laughter. Then the young voice said: 'Cut the lip you ol' goat. Do as I say before we pull the place apart.'

'What's the matter, Kit?' said another gruffer voice.

'The ol' goat's acting awkward. I guess we woke him out of his beauty sleep.'

'What you got in the back old-timer?' said the other. 'Somethin' smells good. Come on, Kit.'

'You keep outa there,' shrilled the old man. 'I got a guest an' he don't like bein' disturbed.'

There was a sound of a scuffle, a sharp cry and a bump. With a tremulous cry the old lady rose to her feet. The stranger stood up as the two men entered, the young one with the raven-black hair and the older man with the thick body and florid face.

'Mornin' boys,' he drawled. 'Havin' a little trouble.'

The younker's eyes widened, his right hand moved. Then he gaped. He was covered by two long barrelled guns. And the handsome face of the man who held them had undergone a transformation.

A brighter light came into the cold eyes, the mobile lips were stretched into a snarl. 'Back, damn you,' he said. 'Back.'

The old lady looked a little shocked. Her peaceful and mannerly guest had suddenly proved himself a wolf in sheep's clothing. She knew enough about gunmen to know an expert when she saw one. And so did the other two men. They backed swiftly. She ran past them and to her husband who rising to his feet was rubbing his jaw.

'The dirty skunks,' he said. Then his attackers came into view shepherded by the lynx-eyed stranger and the old man began to cackle.

'Get their guns, pop,' said the big man.

The oldster obeyed with alacrity while his spouse looked on with a shadow of anxiety on her wrinkled brow.

'Turn around,' snarled the big man. 'An' keep moving.' The two desperadoes wisely, wordlessly, did as they were told. They passed into the street, the stranger behind them, the jubilant hotel-keeper bringing up the rear, the former's two guns clenched in his gnarled fists.

There were three covered wagons drawn up in the street. There were men in their driving seats and a few others gathered around them. They gaped and shifted.

The stranger's deep voice boomed out. 'Up with them, all of yuh. Spread out. Quickly or, by God, I'll start shootin'.'

That authoritative voice transfixed them. Their hands went up, mechanically. All except one pair. The stranger's left-hand Colt boomed. The bold teamster yelled with pain and fell, his shoulder drilled. His hand had never reached his gun.

'That was very foolish,' said the big man. 'I might've killed yuh.' His voice was soft – but surcharged with passion. Then it rose again. 'Spread out, damn you! Spread out I said! . . . Watch 'em pop.'

'Shore thing, son,' said the old man with a toothless leer.

'You two,' said the stranger to Kit and his pard. 'Move aside. Gently, don't get into my line of fire or I might drill you. Get on the end of the line there.'

Very warily the black-haired younker and his blocky companion joined the others before the wagons.

The man jerked a gun at the teamsters on their perches. 'Come on down here with your friends,' he said.

They began to climb down. The one on the first wagon was big and mean-looking. He had red hair and squint eyes. He spoke.

'What's the idea? Is this a hold-up?'

'I'll ask the questions,' said the stranger. 'What's your business?'

'We're buffalo-hunters,' said the other as he landed on the ground. His little eyes watched the two-gun man warily and his suddenly competent looking pard, the old hotel-keeper.

The stranger ran his queer blue eyes along the line of men before the wagon.

'Very few o' yuh look like buffalo-hunters,' he said. 'What've you got in the wagons?'

'Jest provisions. We're goin' huntin' now.'

'How come you touched North Platte? I thought the hunters started from Julesburg. More buffs up that way.'

'We're freelances. My boys don't want to get mixed up with them government contractors from Julesburg.' . . . The redhead man suddenly began to snarl. 'You ask a lotta questions, stranger. If you don't want us here we'll move on. But we'll remember you.'

The other's eyes narrowed. 'You the boss o' this outfit?'

'Yeh.'

'Wal, boss, I'd like to look in them wagons o' yourn . . . Watch 'em, Pop.'

'Shore thing,' The old man looked as if he only wanted a chance to start blasting.

The stranger went closer to the red-headed man. 'Open them flaps,' he said.

'I'll see you . . .'

'Open 'em! I mean business.'

Something in the other's eyes made the teamster blanch. He turned to the wagon. It was then the diversion occurred.

A buck-skin-clad man came out of Cal Buggin's store next-door-but-one to the hotel. There was a gun in his hand. The old lady ran on to the hotel-stoop screaming a warning. The oldster half-turned as the man fired. The slug took him high in the side of the chest, knocking him over. Regardless of danger the old lady flung herself on her knees beside him.

The big stranger was triggering. The new arrival was mowed down before he could fire another shot. Taking his chance the redheaded teamster swung a heavy-booted foot and kicked the big man's legs from under him. As he fell he kicked him again on the head. The stranger's guns spun in the dust. He lay still.

A shotgun boomed and two of the buffalo-hunters cried out, wounded by the spraying buckshot. Fat old store-keeper, Cal Buggins had taken a hand in the proceedings. Further along the street another old-stager came to the door with a gun in each fist. North Platte was having a new lease of life and its ancient inhabitants grasped at it with both hands.

'Get your horses,' bawled the red-headed man. 'Let's get out of here.'

He jumped to his seat. Men ran for their horses. The

scatter-gun boomed again. Some of the men retaliated. But old Cal had taken refuge in his store. The other oldster down the street began firing-off both his guns. Somebody else ran out with a rifle. Another rifle spat from an upstairs window. The denizens of the ghost-town were pretty solid spooks – and they were enjoying themselves. A winged slug knocked a teamster from his perch. He clambered ungainly up again, his right arm dripping blood.

The big stranger lying in the dust began to stir. 'Finish him,' screamed the redhead as he whipped up his horses. A vicious-looking rider drew a bead on the fallen man's head. Cal Buggin's scatter-gun boomed again. The rider stopped most of the charge and was precipitated from his horse with part of his head blown away.

Whips cracked, hooves clattered. The big stranger rose to his knees, hands snaking out for his dusty guns as the cavalcade thundered off down the street, pursued by the wrath and the jubilance of North Platte.

But they left death behind them in the shattered body of one of their own men and in the still, peaceful form of the old hotel-keeper, whose wife sobbed on his chest.

A slit-eyed killer rose from the dust and slid his guns into their greased holsters as he peered after the diminishing dustcloud.

NINE

It was another black Nebraska night and the mountainous Dragon, who seemed almost scared of utter darkness, was cursing and muttering.

'Hold your noise,' growled the half-breed, Longhair, at his side. Dragon flung one last blistering epithet into the starless night and subsided. He could barely see the bobbing backs of Bill Cody and Bucko Martin who were riding a little way in front of him and his companion.

The ground became more rocky and uneven under their horses' feet as they wended their way into the foothills. They began to climb. At length they dismounted from their beasts and led them slowly. Now Longhair took the lead. Half crouching, he did not hesitate much. Bucko wondered how he could find his way in such blackness. Maybe he smelt it. The night was oppressive. Longhair smelt something, and spoke of it. 'Storm comin' up,' he said laconically.

'Well,' said Cody. 'We ought to be near shelter soon – if it ain't already occupied.'

'Quiet,' said Longhair sharply. 'Take it easy. Up along there is where we got ambushed last time.'

'We'd better hobble the horses an' leave 'em here while we go an' reconnoitre,' hissed Cody.

They did this, and continued laboriously on foot. No

shot cleaved the turgid silence, no challenge from the blackness ahead. Longhair led them through a rocky cleft and they descended into the valley below. There was no light, no sound down there. The faint breeze was stopped altogether now, the night seemed suddenly warmer, and even darker. The four men crept closer to the log cabin. They split up: Dragon and Longhair went around back, Cody and Bucko approached the front. Half crouching they reached the log walls and flattened themselves each side of the door.

They drew their guns. It was Bucko who reached out and lifted the latch. Then he kicked the door open. The sound was like a pistol shot in the stillness and Cody cursed under his breath. But Bucko, ever reckless, was already inside the place. Cody followed him. There was no need for caution now. Bucko was blundering about in the back somewhere. Cody heard his muffled swearing. Then his plaintive voice said: 'Shut that goldurned door an' let's have some light.' Then the voice called softly: 'Longhair, Dragon.' There was the sound of another door opening and shutting. So the place had an exit too! 'Where the heck are yer?' said Dragon in a deafening stage-whisper.

Cody shut the door and struck a Lucifer. There was a quick sharp sound in a corner and the hunter started, his other hand reaching across his belly for his gun. The sound stopped. A rat. Only the very human and clumsier sounds of stumbling men could be heard from the other room. Cody's light illuminated the sordid dusty interior then went out. In the other room a flame blossomed. 'I found a lamp,' said Bucko. Cody passed through the communicating door and joined the other three.

Dragon had rolled down the thick blind that covered the small back window. It was an inevitable necessity in a hideout such as this. The four men gazed around them. They were in a sleeping compartment-cum-kitchen. The smell assailed their nostrils of rotten cooking-fat, dirt and stale sweat. There were six bunkers in two tiers round three of the walls and blankets were strewn around the floor as if people slept there too. There was a paraffin-stove on a shelf in a corner and a small dirty table on which were piled various cooking utensils and items of crockery, as well as the remains of a meal. There were a few chairs and a couple of packing-cases. The place was crowded with stuff, too much of it to take in all at once. No wonder the boys had blundered around.

Despite the evidence of it being 'lived-in' the place had a deserted, closed-up look. Probably the gang had not been back since they were chased away the other night. The three buffalo-hunters and the ex-cowboy began to give it a thorough going-over.

It was the lynx-eyed Longhair who made the first find. 'Injuns have been here,' he said. 'I thought there was a lingering smell of 'em.' He wasn't overproud of the savage side of his own ancestry. He held up a buffalo-hide bandeau from around some redskin's brow.

Dragon made a second find and was hugely amused by it. 'Ain't that a beauty?' he said. He held up a yellow-haired scalp, dirty, the dried blood matted to it. Bucko Martin recoiled. 'It won't bite yer,' said Dragon. 'It's an old one. But it's a prize. One o' them red critturs is probably mighty sorry he dropped it.'

'Looks like a woman's,' said Cody. 'A white woman's. Probably came off that wagon-train that was wiped out by the Sioux coupla months ago.' That was past and he was most laconic about it – or at least pretended to be. Although Bucko Martin did not show his feelings either, he was unaccountably moved. He could almost visualize that woman who had been proud of those golden tresses – little more than a girl she would've been when the savages took her. He knew enough about them to know that she was an old woman when she finally died, outraged and tortured . . . maybe his imagination was running away with him. Maybe it hadn't been like that at all, maybe she had died instantly from an arrow or a bullet – even the bullet from the gun of a husband, sweetheart or a friend – and had been scalped afterwards. He hoped it had been like that for her, poor kid . . .

Cody was talking. 'Judging by the traces, them Injuns left in a hurry,' he said. 'I wonder whether they were friends of the bandits – or otherwise.'

'If they were otherwise wouldn't they've made a mess of the place – maybe set fire to it?' Said Bucko.

'There's sense in that. Maybe they were looking for Death an' his men. But why leave in such a hurry. . . ?'

'If they were familiar here maybe they'd be lolling about. Didn't notice the things they dropped . . .'

'I figure they were drunk,' put in Longhair. 'Among the other stinks, I smell whiskey.'

'I guess you've hit it,' said Cody.

Dragon was blundering about in the other rooms seeking fresh spoils. 'Bring the lantern in here,' he said. 'I've pulled down the blind.'

They went into him, Bucko carrying the hurricane-lantern. He placed it on the table in the other room. The table was bare except for a small wooden box on its one corner. It was a dealing-box. Bucko slid aside the shutter at the top and revealed a greasy pack of cards. There were five chairs drawn in careless-fashion around the board as if inviting visitors to sit down and have a nice quiet flutter. There was a cupboard against the wall beside the outer door. Cody opened it. Inside was a row of empty bottles and a few jumbled dirty glasses and thick earthenware mugs. Against the opposite wall was a long bench. Beneath this they found a bottle containing a few dregs of whiskey. Before the bench was a cracked, pot-bellied stove, its lower vent spilling cold ashes over the tin plate beneath it. There was nothing else.

'Looks to me like that gang didn't come back after we chased 'em. They figured it was too risky I guess,' said Cody. 'But in the meantime a bunch of Injuns've been here – friends of their's maybe, looking for 'em. Probably they waited a bit, maybe they drunk what was left of the whiskey . . .'

'I think our boys took all that,' interrupted Dragon.

'Well, maybe the Injuns brought some whiskey with 'em,' said Cody with crushing irony. 'Maybe it's the Injuns who are sellin' it to the whites.'

'Horsefeathers!' jeered Dragon. The way he said it made it sound like the most shocking and bloodcurdling of expletives. 'I guess the Injuns hung around a bit waiting for their dirty white partners then took their hook,' said Cody.

'An' not so long ago either I figure,' said Longhair. 'I don't like this place. It stifles me. I vote we get out. I guess I can pick up the trail.'

'This'll make good shelter when it rains,' said Bucko facetiously.

Longhair contemptuously ignored the remark. 'I vote we get out,' he repeated.

'I second that,' said Dragon and strode to the door.

'Wait a minute,' said Cody. 'Douse the light . . .' He broke off as the door was suddenly flung open. Two Indians burst in, rifles in their hands pointed at the white men. Painted red faces appeared at the window, the glass was shattered, the muzzles of two more rifles came through.

Dragon cursed, reaching. 'Hold it,' said Cody. 'We ain't got a chance. Maybe we can pow-wow.'

Dragon shrugged and desisted. 'Maybe,' he grunted. But even he could see Cody's wisdom. No use in throwing their lives away without a try at something. The back-door crashed open. Moccasined feet padded and more Indians came through from the kitchen. They were coming in both ways now, a dozen or more of them so far – and all with new shiny rifles. They were silent, moving almost like the well-trained soldiers in whose hands those rifles should have been.

Soon the four white men were surrounded by their stinking red hides, their hideously-painted faces with malignant black eyes. The ring broke as the savages moved aside deferentially for their chief. He was old and clad only in informal dress, a buffalo-robe around his thin shoulders, copper rings on his arms, a single eagle's feather transfixing the greasy top-knot on his shaven pate.

Cody held up his hand in the peace-sign. The chief ignored it. He merely grunted a few words in his own language. The braves moved forward again and seized the palefaces. All four of them fought, Dragon terribly, like a huge bear, throwing screeching red men in all directions. Bucko Martin tried to get at his gun but his arms were pinioned to his side from behind. Another red man, with a face painted, whirled like a catherine-wheel, gibbered at him, his hot breath fanning the cowboy's face.

Cody struck out right and left with his fists, clearing a space for himself. Then he, too, reached for his gun. His wrists were caught and wrenched behind him, a bony knee was ground into his back. Another savage caught a handful of his long hair and pulled his head back, back until the hunter's throat was stretched and bared.

Wriggling and spitting like a diamond-backed rattler, Longhair broke away from the clutching hands and drew his knife. He had ripped one savage's belly open and almost slashed another's arm off before they finally beat him to his knees, and unconsciousness, with the butts of their rifles. One brave had grasped his hair, his knife ready preparatory to the lightning circular motion of scalping when the chief rapped a sharp guttural command.

The other white men were also stunned into submission, Dragon bleeding from a gash across his eye, then hauled to their feet again and hustled forward to confront the chief. He looked them over speculatively, probably devising in his heathen mind terrible tortures that would change them from fighting men into crying animals.

Hoofbeats sounded outside, clattered to a stop; then footsteps, the door was flung open. The braves parted to let the new arrivals through to the centre of the circle.

'Death Ordey!' panted Cody.

'Hallo, Will Cody,' said the cadaverous bandit-leader. 'Nice tuh see yuh again. Longhair – Dragon – an' the new boy . . .'

'You dirty stinkun' renegade,' snarled Dragon. 'You son of a cow . . .' He started forward, almost grasped Ordey before he was drawn back. The skeleton-man hit him across the forehead, making the blood spurt afresh from the wound above the eye.

Dragon struggled madly, speechless, only strangled cries and grunts coming from his writhing lips. His eyes glared crazily from amid the curly black hair of his beard and moustache and the thick tendrils of his tousled head-locks. The Indian chief, who stood beside the bandit-leader, started back a little in awe. So did his followers behind him, some of them giving little exclamations of dismay. A crazy man, possessed by devils, was something that their black, superstitious hearts recoiled from.

Ordey thought and acted swiftly. He drew his gun, swung it and hit Dragon a terrible blow on the head. The big hunter slumped unconscious, blood matting his beard and staining the front of his shirt. Ordey spoke a few rapid

words in dialect to the chief, who made a grunting reply
and nodded understandingly.

Bucko Martin was glaring at the cadaverous leader with
almost as much ferocity as Dragon had done. He was
trembling with impotent fury and frustration. Here, a few
yards away from him, was the man he hated, the man he
had sworn to kill and his own arms were held in the steel-
like clutch of savage fingers, he was weaponless, sick,
dazed, his fury only making him feel worse.

Longhair, held on his feet by stalwart bucks, was still
half-unconscious. Cody, erect again, was staring past
Ordey at the other white men who were moving through
the Indian ranks to join him.

'Slim Jackson,' he said. 'Ackroyd, La Brue, Pete Kramer.
I thought you were dead . . .'

A horrible grin lit up the bandit-leader's skull-like white
face. 'Well, they ain't,' he said.

'I'm beginning to see daylight,' said Cody.

'You won't ever see daylight again, Will,' leered Ordey.
'We've got a little all-night jamboree worked out fer you
an' your boys.'

'You slimy scum,' said Cody. 'I guessed you were behind
this new Injun trouble.'

Ordey laughed. 'You guessed right, Almighty Will,' he
said. 'By the way, do you like the nice new rifles my red
brothers've got? They've only just come through. There's
a couple o' cases o' whiskey too, stashed away for us to
celebrate with after our plans are carried through. I'd like
to tell you about those plans, Will.'

'Go ahead,' said Cody. 'It'll be an experience for me –
learning how your sick crazy mind works.'

That thrust went home. Ordey bared his teeth, looking
more like a skeleton than ever. Then he recovered
himself.

'Well, I'll tell you,' he said. 'Tonight in this valley there's a big meeting of all the Indians in the territory. Already you can hear them coming. Listen.'

But already the prisoners were aware of the increasing sound of movement from outside, the clattering of the unshod hooves of mustangs, the clink of steel against rock, the guttural muttering of savage voices.

'When they are all here,' continued Ordey, 'We are going to raid the U.P. line at a given point.' He paused. 'You didn't know there was a train comin' thru' tonight did you Will? It's a secret even from a mighty man like you. But I knew about it.'

Not by the merest flicker of an eyelash did Cody reveal his shocked surprise, the sudden cold prickling of horror.

'Yes,' said Ordey. 'General Casement is coming back by train instead of sneaking along the comparatively safe river trail by coach. Very bold of him isn't it? He's trying to be clever you see. He's bringing the U.P. payroll, an' more soldiers.' Ordey chuckled. He was enjoying himself; his white bony face shone with horrible glee. 'It was a mighty big secret, Will. Funny me knowin' it an' not you ain't it?'

'You've got somebody workin' with you in town,' burst out Cody. 'Somebody who can get to know about these things. Somebody pretty big maybe.'

'Maybe,' echoed the other. 'Maybe I'll tell you about that later. But first of all I want to finish telling you all about my plans for you an' your friends. My red brothers want to treat you like they treat all their prisoners. I think they'd even worked out a few special tortures for you. But I've persuaded them out of it. I'm sick of mere torture – it's beginning to pall.' Ordey paused with assumed languidness like an actor about to speak his most dramatic lines. 'I don't think such men as you should be treated in this sordid way. I think you should go out in a blaze of glory. No death is too good for the Mighty Cody and his fighting friends. So I, personally, have devised a special ending for you. Ain't you grateful to me, Will, for bein' so considerate?'

Cody did not answer. His face was marble-like. It was Bucko Martin who spat out the words. 'I'd like to go out with my two guns in my hands facin' you and your mob of stinking swine who call themselves white. But that would-n't be the end you picked for me would it you crawlin', gutless heathen?'

'Your cowboy friend speaks well,' said Ordey as he looked at the young man.

Bucko cleared his throat and, with a little jerk of his head, spat out its contents. They spread on Ordey's face; a thin line of spittle ran, and dripped from his chin. The face became demoniacal; Ordey started forward, his hands extended like claws. Then again he recovered himself and, lifting his boot kicked the young cowboy savagely in the stomach. With a choking cry, Bucko crum-pled up, his senses leaving him as he retched.

Ordey wiped the mess from his face with his sleeve. 'Pity,' he said. 'Two men out. I did want you all to hear my little tale.'

Longhair had regained full consciousness now. He said 'I'm listenin' to yuh now, Mr Lawyer Ordey. I'm gettin' eddicated.'

The other said: '. . . to better the glory you even jest in the face of Death.' He cackled aloud at his own pun. His men joined in. The redskins looked blank, their chief annoyed. As if to placate him Ordey made more threaten-ing gestures in the direction of the prisoners and gave the phlegmatic old savage an ingratiating leer.

'My brother, Red Cloud, and I will lead the raid,' he said. 'And in the forefront too will be you and your friends, Will Cody. You'll be tied to your horses, stripped to the waist, painted and with feathers in your hair. Red Cloud wants to scalp you alive first. You have such beautiful locks, all of you. I shall probably help him to do it an' keep your scalp for myself, Will, keep it in memory of you . . . You will ride to glory and your bodies will be left with the rest. When you're found, your bonds cut, they'll think you were renegades who led the raid.' His voice became thoughtful. 'I don't think it'll be a good thing to scalp you after all. It'll look more realistic if you're found just as you are, made up like Injuns – shot down while leading your red brothers on a train massacre. The *crowning glory*.' He began to laugh again, then checked himself with a sidelook at Red Cloud.

'You're a ravin' lunatic,' said Cody. 'You won't get away with all this.'

'And why shouldn't I, Will? Why shouldn't I?'

The words echoed in the brains of the prisoners like the knell of doom. Yes, *why shouldn't he?*

Bucko and Dragon, both tough as they make 'em, had regained consciousness. The Indians busied themselves in tying the prisoners' hands behind them and looping rope-halters around their necks. Then they were shepherded outside.

The valley seemed to be jammed with savages. They were unusually silent but a primitive, guttural murmur went up as they saw the paleface prisoners. A fire had begun to flame in the middle of the circle around which the press of them was the greatest. Buffeted and reviled from all sides the prisoners were forced into this circle so that they could be seen by all. The firelight gleamed upon them and, from the assembled redskins in the darkness came a collective, blood-chilling sound like a harsh sigh. The prisoners were pulled into line by cruel jerks on the halter-ropes that nearly throttled them.

'Line up,' said Death Ordey. 'Let 'em have a look at you.' Then he turned again and began to chatter and gesticulate to Red Cloud.

Other chiefs and sub-chiefs in war-paint and full regalia

began to move into the circle of firelight and examine the prisoners. They prodded them and pinched them, pulling their hair experimentally, twisting their ears and noses, spitting into their faces, uttering deep, delighted cries like cruel children.

Suddenly Death Ordey raised himself on his toes, his tall terribly-emaciated figure etched against the firelight, his arms waving in the air. 'Listen, everybody,' he shouted.

Most of the savages did not understand what he said but the authorative voice and gestures of this strange, corpse-like paleface who rode with their chiefs, made them silent.

Old Red Cloud strode to his white brother's side and likewise held up his hands. Then he began to speak. His voice was cracked, guttural, but still strong. At first he stood immobile his arms folded upon his chest then, as interest quickened and stirred his listeners, he began to gesticulate. His voice became shriller, his words became faster, interspersed with gasps. His listeners began to shriek or utter deep cries. He was whipping them up in to a frenzy. Then when his voice ceased and his lean old body slumped in lethargy, the dance began.

The flames roared as more logs were thrown on the fire, sparks flutterer like stars above the valley. The circle of firelight widened and around it in circles the shrieking savages capered. The chief and sub-chiefs kept to the inside rim. Every now and then one of them would break from the line and do a few improvised shuffling steps to reach the prisoners. Then he would caper in front of them, administering blows from time to time. When he wheeled away another speedily took his place. They were cruelly systematic, their blows hurt but did not mark too badly. That was probably due to Ordey who stood leering watchfully near by.

Another point the prisoners noticed was the absence of thudding war-drums. The savages made their own beat with their moccasined feet and their sharp shrill cries.

Drum-beats would carry far on the still air and they did not want to give away their warlike intentions to listening white sentinels.

'This is a mighty well-planned jamboree,' said Longhair.

'White devil's work again,' said Bucko. He was bruised and battered, but undaunted; his courage, and his hatred for that thin, yellow-faced monster still burned within him. Maybe before they finished him off he would have a chance to get his hands around that scrawny throat and choke the life from that rotten shell. It was a forlorn hope, but with it he buoyed up his spirits and his nerve. He ignored the sharp blows; the capering screeching Indians with their painted bodies and hideous faces gleaming in the firelight looked like demons from the uttermost pit of hell but they failed to awe and terrify him. He'd never been scared. Right now he hadn't a lot to live for except his vengeance. He ignored the possibility that he might die with it unsatisfied and his hate filled his body like an ever-increasing ball of strength and fury.

Red Cloud joined Death and his bunch of men and they pow-wowed for a while. Then the old Indian chief left them and moved among the other chiefs and sub-chiefs. One by one they moved out of the circle and infiltrated themselves into the jigging crowd. Gradually the shrieking and thumping of feet became less. The dancing ceased altogether. The babbling died down and almost silently the men began to get their horses. The time had come.

Red Cloud and three more younger sub-chiefs gathered around the prisoners. At a guttural command from the old Indian the young braves tore the shirts from the backs of the white men.

Another Indian appeared with a bowl of sickly-looking warpaint, a mysterious villainous smelling concoction. He began to daub this thickly on the bodies and faces of the prisoners, drawing patterns and circles with his fingers.

Death Ordey joined the group. 'When they've finished with you nobody'll know whether you're white men, black men, red men or Chinee men,' he cackled.

To finish the job the redskins put ragged bandeaus around the white mens' heads and decorated them with feathers. But even then Ordey wasn't satisfied. 'Let's have the job done properly,' he said. 'Slice their britches.' He turned and jabbered to Red Cloud. The old Indian gave more orders. The braves drew their knives and slashed the prisoners' trousers until their legs and knees showed through the rents and their buttocks were almost bare.

'You're gonna be mighty uncomfortable, boys,' said Ordey. 'Perched in your skin on top o' barebacked nags. But you'll look like real Injuns.'

'I note you didn't slice your britches, you yeller snake,' said Longhair. 'I guess your bones 'ud rattle.'

Many of the savages wore trousers, mostly captured cavalry britches but, to facilitate a better grip on their ponies, they had slashed the legs to ribbons and cut the seats away altogether. If they had not looked so unspeakably hideous in their warpaint, they would have been comical.

The prisoners were hauled on to the bare backs of bony half-wild mustangs and tied there. Each had a halter round his neck, the other end of the rope held by one of Ordey's men.

Some semblance of formation was evolved from the chaos and the cavalcade began to ride from the valley.

The ribbed back of his Indian pony began to rub the skin from Bucko Martin's bruised limbs. He bounced like a rag doll on the unfamiliar perch and with each jerk the rough hemp around his throat almost throttled him. He sunk his head on his bare painted chest . . .

TEN

The tall rider who sat so erect in the saddle on his big, nigger-brown stallion, reined-in at the ranch and looked upwards at its sagging archway. In faded black paint on the weatherbeaten wooden cross-piece was inscribed: Pete Crow Ranch. The letters were at least a foot and a half high but cracked and peeling, in places, half-obliterated. The archway had doubtless once been a very imposing affair but now it sagged to the peril of all who passed beneath it, and presented a very neglected and dilapidated appearance. As was the custom, there was no gate, the trail led right through and the rider could see the cluster of ranch-houses, the outhouses and barns and fences straight in front of him. He drew a packet of cheroots and a book of matches from his vest pocket. He etched a brimstone streak on the right-hand wooden pillar and lit up. Then, drawing furiously, so that the smoke, lifted by the breeze, floated in small clouds behind him, he continued nonchalantly onwards.

A rider broke away from the ranch-buildings sending his horse at a trot along the trail. The stranger's back stiffened but his air of nonchalance did not leave him. He checked his horse's restiveness with a pat of his hand on the glossy neck. The gap between the two riders lessened as the second one came up more rapidly.

He was dressed in conventional cowboy garb but his face seemed to belie his appearance of an outdoor man; it was unnaturally pale and puffy. His pale little eyes scrutinized the tall handsome stranger. He reined-in. His left sleeve was rolled up and the arm laced with white bandages. 'Howdy,' he said.

The stranger took his cheroot from his mouth. 'Howdy,' he replied.

'Can I help you?' said the other. His tone was affable but his eyes were suspicious.

'I'm lookin' fer a job. Anythin' on a ranch.'

The other's little eyes still showed that suspicious interest. He leaned forward a little in his saddle. 'Your face looks familiar. Ain't I seen you from somewhere? Where you from?'

'I came here after a job, not to answer questions,' said the stranger, without rancour. 'Still, I guess it don't do you nor me any harm to tell yuh. I've punched cattle all over the States but came originally from the Panhandle. I wuz there last, too. Working for a spread called the Cross W, owned by of Hank Maltby. Know him?'

'No. I've only been to the Panhandle once in my life an' that wasn't for long. Maybe I've seen you other places though. What's your handle?'

'Maybe you'd better tell me yourn first,' said the stranger, still without rancour. 'Tell me also what you think gives you the right to be the interlocutor-man around here.'

The shadow of a smile crossed the other's pasty visage. 'My name's Dick Boynton,' he said. 'I'm the straw-boss around here. I'm responsible for the hands. I'm the man who gives the jobs out.'

'Oh,' said the stranger. 'Then you're the man I wanted to see. Glad tuh know yuh, Mr Boynton. My name's Limes, Jake Limes.'

Boynton shook his head. 'Can't recollect the name. But I could've sworn I'd seen you some place before.'

'I can't recollect at all,' said Limes. 'But it's likely.'

'Have you been in Julesburg?' said Boynton.

'Nope. If I didn't pick up nothin' here I wuz figurin' on riding that way and gettin' me a job with the railroad. I hear they can allus use a man who knows how to handle himself. Though I'd sooner scrap for a cow-outfit, if need be, than any pesky Iron Horse.' His mobile lips quirked in a smile that lit up his handsome face, but did not seem to make much impression on the level clarity of his eyes.

'You're a two-gun man I see,' said Boynton.

'Yeh. An' I don't wear 'em for ornament.'

'Well,' said Boynton. 'We're pestered by Injuns an' horse-thieves around here, as you can imagine.'

'Yeh.'

'We can always use a good gunny, provided he's a good cowhand as well.'

'I kin prove that, Mr Boynton.'

'All the boys call me Dick,' said the other magnaminously . . . 'Look, I gotta ride out on business now. You go in an' see the boss. He's around the ranch someplace. Tell him I sent yuh.'

'Thanks – Dick.'

'It'll be all right,' said Boynton with a wave of his hand. 'I can use you. So-long, Jake.'

'So-long, Dick. You've got yuh a boy. Anythin' I kin do . . .'

As they passed each other the two men exchanged glances and Boynton felt suddenly chilled. Here was a fighting-man who would have no mercy on anyone who stood in his way.

Jake Limes met an old-timer who told him the boss, Pete Crow was out on the back veranda of the ranch-house. The tall man left his horse at the corral, and walked around the big frame building that, like everything around it, bore traces of neglect.

He reached the back veranda and saw the oldish man who was gently swaying in a rocker and gazing out to the windswept range, and the gleaming ribbon where the River Platte bisected it.

The man's lined grey face was petulant in thought and at first he did not see the newcomer whose bootheels had made no sound in the dust. Then suddenly his head jerked as if on a spring, his eyes looked almost frightened, he half-rose from his chair.

'Mighty sorry I startled you, suh,' said Limes. He walked up the steps on to the veranda and looked down at the spare man in the chair.

The older man looked back at him and spoke in a petulant voice. 'Well, what d'you want?'

The tall man's cold eyes took on an almost mild expression. 'You're Mr Crow I take it, suh,'

'I am,' the other snapped out the words nervously.

'Your straw-boss, Mr Boynton, sent me tuh find you. My name's Jake Limes. I'm after a job. Anythin' on a ranch I kin do – bin a cowboy ever since I wuz a nipper. Mr Boynton says all right ef'n you . . .' The man paused diffidently.

'Well, if Mr Boynton says all right I guess you're hired,' rapped Crow. 'But don't come creeping around corners like that again.'

'No, suh.' The cowboy cuffed his hat awkwardly to the back of his head.

'You'd better go see the cook – maybe he'll give you a cup of coffee or somethin'. See Boynton when he comes back.' Crow looked nervously past the new man. The interview was at an end.

'Yes, suh,' said Jake Limes. He stamped his feet a little as he walked away. Crow did not seem to notice this pantomime. He was staring petulantly in front of him once more as if something out there fascinated yet annoyed him.

The cook proved to be a small pot-bellied amiable Texan. He was mighty interested to learn that Limes had come from the Panhandle and, while the latter got outside a mug of hot coffee and some apple-pie, they exchanged reminiscences. The stranger knew his Panhandle all right.

He asked the usual 'new fish' questions about the ranch and its people, and the cook, who evidently loved gossip, besides having taken a liking to this tall, handsome critter, was happy to oblige him with little harmless anecdotes. By his account most everything was left to the discretion of Dick Boynton who, despite his appearance, was a good man at his job. His looks were doubtless due to his guts or something. The cook couldn't remember him ever being any different. But then he himself had only been at the place about seven months.

'D'yuh like it here?' said Limes.

'Yeh, it's all right.'

'Any trouble?'

'We useter have Injuns an' all sorts when the U.P. was goin' through here. That wuz when I fust got here. But since then its been quite peaceful.'

'Ever seen any buff'lers up this way? I've only ever seen me about a couple o' the beasts.'

'Well, if its buff'lers you want to see, up along the South Platte is the best place. Thousands of 'em. Not as we don't get small herds down here sometime. We do.'

'Any huntin' done round here?'

'Well, yes, now you come to speak of it I guess there is. There's a bunch of hunters call here from time to time. Same bunch. Friends o' the boss's I guess . . .' The cook paused. For the first time his round amiable face assumed a suspicious look. 'A cowboy don't want to go around with no buff'lers,' he said. 'What was you doin' – thinkin' of joinin' up with a bunch of hunters?'

'Well, I had thought about it. If I hadn't got taken on here I should've tried to join up with some. Be a change maybe – I've been a cowpuncher all my life . . . I guess you think I'm loco. I guessed there was nothin' else for it though. Now, o'course, I'm not worried.'

The cook grinned, his good humour restored. 'You stick around cows, pardner,' he said. 'They ain't so treacherous as them other critturs.' He turned to his stove. 'Guess I'd better be rustlin' up some chow. The boys'll be ridin' in soon an' they can be mighty nasty if they ain't fed properly. Jest take it easy. You can go in an' have your meal with 'em when they come.'

'Sure,' said the other. 'Ef'n I've got room. This is mighty fine pie.'

The cook spoke again, his back turned to his listener. His voice was pitched on a cheerful note, but there was an undercurrent of something else. 'If I wuz you I shouldn't ask too many questions around here. You won't be popular if you do an' you might not be asked to stay. I guess they on'y keep me 'cos I see nothin' and, if I see somethin', don't say nothin'.'

'An' because you can cook,' said Limes. He made no further comment.'

Presently he rose. 'I guess I'll go an' see to my hoss,' he said.

The cook jerked a greasy thumb. 'Stables are the other side o' the ranch-house.'

'Thanks, I'll see yuh.'

When Limes came away from the stables the boys were riding in. He followed them to the mess-hut and with easy charm buttonholed a few of them and introduced himself. They were a hard-looking bunch.

Limes' neighbour at the table was a brutish, black-

jowled individual, who went by the name of 'Batty.' He had
a swelling red bruise on his temple. It seemed that a frisky
steer had knocked him from his horse. The anecdote, with
embellishments and would-be witty asides, was recounted
over and over again across the table while Batty sat in
lumpish silence. He was evidently a bit weak in the upper
storey and was quite used to this kind of treatment, both
from the stock and from his own pards.

'Steers jest naturally hate Batty like pizen,' said one
lean, sneering individual. 'He ain't no more use around
stock than Mabel with her combs off.'

Everybody laughed, including Limes. Batty took no
more notice of him than he did the others. Then a loud
voice said 'I cain't think why he's kept here. 'Cept that he's
crazy enough to plug anybody Boynton tells him to. He
loves Mister Boynton. Don't you Batty?'

There was a dead silence. The man who had caused it
clapped his lips together tightly, as if to stop his tongue
wagging further, and looked sheepish. Everybody was
looking at Batty.

The stranger, Limes he had said his name was, and he
looked like a gunman, did not appear to be unduly interested. He was attacking his soup. But Batty had come alive.
He was glaring at the loud-mouthed man and growling
deep in his throat like an enraged animal. Suddenly his
hand appeared above the table. The lamplight glinted on
the barrel of the gun it held.

Limes whirled in his seat. His hand grasped Batty's wrist
and wrenched his arm upwards. The gun went off. The
bullet ploughed a furrow high in the log-wall opposite.
They wrestled for a second, Batty growling and showing
his teeth. Then Limes hit him beneath the jaw. He
sprawled backwards from the bench and hit the back of
his head on the wall. He sat there, conscious, but his eyes
glazed, his expression vacuous.

The loud-mouthed man had gone white.

'Thanks, friend,' he said.

'I couldn't sit here while he shot somebody,' said Limes. He looked at Batty. 'Will he be all right?'

'I guess so,' said one man. 'We'll watch him. He'll probably forget what's happened an' get back up to the table like a little lamb.'

Limes appropriated the gun to make sure. But, sure enough, a few minutes later Batty sat down again and attacked his cold soup furiously as if he had only just arrived and wanted to catch up with the others. Covert glances were thrown at the fast stranger from all sides. He ignored them. He was a cool customer, the cowhands concluded.

As they were leaving the hut the loud-mouthed man nudged him. 'Don't say anythin' to Boynton about that little ruckus, will yuh, pard? It'll only cause trouble.'

'I won't,' Limes promised.

To show his gratitude the loud-mouthed man took Limes to the bunk-house and pointed out to him the only vacant bunk.

'It belonged to Mick O'Dowd,' he said. 'He got killed . . .' The speaker shut his lips tightly again, obviously afraid of saying too much once more.

Limes didn't seem to notice the abrupt silence. He looked around the bunkhouse and sniffed.

'You'll get used to the stink,' said loud-mouth with unconscious humour. 'It'll be wuss when we bed down. It's that Batty agin, mostly. Last time he had a bath wuz when we tossed him in the Platte. He's about due for another duckin' soon I guess.'

'I've slept in worse dumps,' said Limes.

The stink didn't seem to bother him none later on when he sat smoking and playing poker with a bunch of the boys. His chair was tilted back against the wall. He had unobtrusively insisted on having that particular one and at least two of the boys had exchanged significant glances. They knew the signs. He still wore his guns too, whereas most of them had taken their gunbelts off and slung them on their bunks. He played poker perfectly, his handsome face as impassive as a Chinese idol's, his blue eyes cold and expressionless.

They gambled for dimes and the new man had a couple of little stacks beside him when the door opened and Dick Boynton looked in. His pale gaze swept the room and came to rest on the poker-table and the tall man who faced him across it.

'I see you've settled in all right, Jake,' he said.

'Sure, Dick.'

'An' taking the boys for a ride already by the look of things.' They smiled thinly at each other as some of the others guffawed.

Then Boynton took his leave.

Limes made a clean-up that night, thereby earning the respect of those hard cases (whose main recreation was gambling), all except a few disgruntled ones who hinted among themselves that there had been some 'sharping' done somewhere. They kept out of earshot of the new man when they made their insinuations, nevertheless.

By the morning, when he rode out with the rest, he had been more or less accepted by most. They chaffed him about his luck and challenged him to another flutter that night so they could have their revenge.

'Are you as lucky around cows?' said one of them with a significant glance in the brutish Batty's direction.

'Can't say that I am,' said Limes.

This proved to be somewhat of an understatement. He may have had the mannerisms of a professional gunman and the luck, or otherwise, of a born gambler, but he was certainly no great shakes as a cowboy. He was almost as bad as the half-witted, clumsy Batty, but it was significant that the boys did not venture to rib him about it. What the heck! Boynton probably had totally different things in mind for him than merely roping steers, branding, and other sordid tasks. They noted that when attempting these operations he wore pigskin gloves. He did not remove them all day. Maybe that was one reason his poker was so slick again that evening. Once more he cleaned-up.

Before he retired more than one man noted that he tucked a gun under his pillow, within reach of his hand, before he composed himself for sleep.

Many of them sat up in the darkness having a final smoke and jawing softly. Maybe Limes didn't notice them when he rose from his bunk once more for he started when one of them spoke to him.

'It's mighty close in here,' he said. 'I guess I ain't acclimatized to this neck o' the woods yet. I'll go outside an' get me a smoke.'

He put on his boots once more, and his gunbelt. He sidled out of the bunkhouse.

He shut the door behind him and, after walking slowly forward a few paces, stopped and lit a cheroot. He meandered around, seemingly aimless. He did not once turn to see if he was being watched.

His perambulations took him around the corner of the bunkhouse. There he could not be seen. He began to move a little faster, but still acted nonchalantly – nothing else but a man out for a cool stroll and a smoke. He reached the wagon track that led beneath the archway and out across the range. Then he began to retrace his steps, his eyes bent thoughtfully on the ground.

He left the trail at the point where the marks of iron-rimmed wheels veered and went across the turf. They were just distinguishable. A funny tack for a wagon to take: it didn't seem to lead any place. Limes followed it aimlessly.

It led him to a tumbledown, disused feed-barn. He dropped the stub of his cheroot and ground it beneath his heel. He walked to the sagging double-doors of the barn and pushed them. He discovered they were padlocked. He took a claspknife fron his pocket and snapped it open.

The thin blade was approaching the lock when it's owner suddenly whirled, holding it like a dagger in front of him.

'Drop it,' said a voice. 'Unless you want me to plug yuh.'

Limes dropped the knife. The man with the gun came nearer. It was Dick Boynton.

'I thought from the start you wuz a snooper,' said the straw-boss. 'You looked like a trouble-shooter. What are you – a lawman?'

'What's the idea, Dick?' said the other. 'I wuz jest havin' a stroll an' a smoke. I ain't snoopin'. I guess I was jest curious. What the heck's eatin' yuh all of a sudden?'

'Keep them hands still,' snarled Boynton. 'You ain't foolin' me. Any funny moves an I'll let you have it.'

The other stood perfectly still, his hands dangling loosely at his sides.

Boynton said: 'I ought to plug you right now but I guess I'd better take you along to the boss. Turn around.' The other complied. 'Now move. To the ranch-house. The back way.'

Limes began to walk. Boynton said softly. 'I wish I could remember where I seen you before.'

'You must have a very poor memory,' said Limes. 'I can remember it quite well. For a moment the other day I thought you'd recognized me.'

'What yuh gettin' at?' said the straw-boss sharply. 'Who are you?'

Limes said softly: 'It was in Abilene you saw me. You didn't call yourself Boynton then.'

No professional actor could have spoken the line more dramatically or with such devastating effect. The tall man heard the other gasp and he folded up, went down on his knees, his body twisting. The slug took his hat off. Both his guns seemed to leap in his hands. Boynton never had a chance to press trigger again; he only had a split second to feel horror and surprise before two slugs crashed into his brain.

Limes ran to the stables. He cursed savagely as he fumbled his saddle in the darkness. Then he was astride the nigger-brown stallion and sweeping through the door.

Men were running from the bunkhouse. Upright in the saddle, clinging to the horse with his knees, Limes fired both guns again. A man screamed. The runners scattered. The rider galloped on. Some men ran for their horses. Others bent over the writhing figure of their companion on the ground.

ELEVEN

The war-party rode steadily through the night. The savages were silent, conserving their passion and resting their vocal chords for the feast of babel and slaughter that lay ahead. Far to the right of them lights flashed dimly. That was Julesburg, the end of the track that brought the hated Iron Horse. But this time they ignored it.

They were moving along an old buffalo-trail. To the right of them was rising ground, its blackness melting into the murk of the sky.

The band of renegades at the head of the column were quite jubilantly talkative, mostly throwing jeers at the four bedaubed prisoners in their midst. Sometimes the prisoners retaliated, but most of the time they were silent. Maybe they hoped for a miracle.

Whether they did or not – *it came!*

Over the rise beside the old buffalo-trail came a horde of flying screeching demons – with such force and suddenness to shock and petrify any unwarned human, red or white. They cut like a tidal wave into the front ranks of the party. The prisoners felt their halter-ropes miraculously part and they were free, carried along like flotsam on the crest of the wave, buffeted and deafened, but free!

Bucko Martin swayed on the ribbed bare back of his horse. A savage rode beside him. The knife in his hand flashed. Instinctively Bucko flinched. But the knife only swept behind him and parted the bonds at his wrists. Bucko almost cried out aloud at the bubbling agony of returning circulation. He almost fell from his mount, a muscular arm held him up. Then the arms were taken away; he managed to bring his hands round in front of him. He clung desperately to the scraggy mane of his mustang. Oh, for a saddle; or even a horse-blanket.

He was bewildered and half-stunned. He had been snatched out of the very palms of one mob of savages by the hands of another bunch, although a much smaller one. Why? And why had his bonds been cut? He tried to twist his head and look for his three partners but so great was the erratic pace of his mustang and so jumbled were his faculties that it seemed he was surrounded only by a sea of tossing, shining bodies – and in his nostrils, like a physical thing, was the stinking tang of Indian flesh.

His ears were deafened and his teeth set on edge by the never-ending screeching but, above all, he thought he heard the rattling of shots. He gave himself up entirely to whatever sprite of Fate had hold of him and crouched low on the pony's back with his arms, like any raw tenderfoot's as he rode a bronc for the first time, draped lovingly round the beast's neck. He hung on like grim death while the little creature went like a rocket, rocking and bouncing, until Bucko's bare flesh was lacerated and bruised and he felt as if every bone in his body was broken. He was not nicknamed Bucko for nothing but right now he'd swop this devilish beast for two killer stallions, a saddle and a pair of strong pants.

After what seemed countless hours he realised their pace had slackened. With a superhuman effort he drew himself erect in the saddle. He even grinned painfully to himself and gave the mustang a sly kick in the ribs, a reminder that the man on top, despite the creature's efforts, was still all in one piece. For sheer guts and staying power he had never ridden the like of this half-savage little Indian pony.

He looked around him. On all sides were Indians, naked to the waist and with feathers in their hair, but all wearing cavalry breeches. Many of them had cartridge-loaded bandoliers slung over their muscular shoulders and across their deep chests. Bucko had all his wits about him now and he realized who these savages were. He had fallen into a detachment of the famous Pawnee scouts, those red men who were hereditary enemies of the Sioux and Cheyennes and staunch allies of the palefaces. They were just as savage, just as cruel, many of them had drip-ping scalps at their belts, but there was something about their orderly silence now, the way they kept their ranks, the way they carried themselves in the saddle, that spoke of an added discipline that other redskins of the plains sadly lacked. A dozen Pawnees in battle were more deadly than three dozen erratic Cheyennes.

Bucko saw Cody, his leonine head bent on his chest. 'Bill!' he shouted.

The buffalo-leader looked up and then began to worm his horse through the ranks towards the cowboy.

He reached his side. 'I jest sort of woke up,' he said. 'Gosh, I'm glad you're still alive.'

'That makes two of us. I'm glad to see you're still all in one piece old-timer. Where's Dragon an' Longhair?'

'I guess they're further back somewhere . . . This is like a miracle ain't it? I've been in tight spots before. But never one like that one. I'd begun to figure it was the last of 'em all. An' then this happened. There's only one man who could be responsible for the coup like this one an' he'll be up ahead I guess. Come on we'll find him.'

A rather bewildered cowboy followed the buffalo-hunter as he broke from the ranks and rode forward.

At the head of the column they came upon three soldiers. 'Major North,' ejaculated Cody. 'You're a sight for sore eyes. You certainly saved our bacon.'

The spare man whom he had addressed, turned in the saddle. 'You're a lucky man, Cody,' he said. 'We were coming back from Fort Kearney when we saw the glow of the fire in the hills and heard the yelling. I sent a couple of my men on the scout and they spotted you. Things have been pretty quiet at the fort, my Pawnees were glad of some action. All we had to do was to trail you and keep out of sight till we saw a favourable opportunity.'

'Just like that,' said Cody admiringly.

'We're suttinly indebted to you, suh,' said the cowboy.

'This is Bucko Martin, Major,' said Cody. 'Come all the way from the Pecos to take the tiger by the tail and swing him ... Bucko – meet Major Frank North of the US Cavalry.'

Bucko shook a lean, vice-like hand. He'd heard of the Major. Who hadn't? Frank North, fighting man supreme, little god of the Pawnee scouts, was already, in his own time, a legend of the West whose fame had swept the length and breadth of a continent. He was introduced to the Major's companions, Captain Brian Plumb, a young subaltern, and Corporal Lem McDougal, a hard-bitten old-timer in buckskin. Lem was known to the Indians as Big Firestick because of the huge, ancient Sharps rifle he carried, and his almost uncanny proficiency with it.

Behind them a voice boomed: 'Will! Bucko!'

They turned, and Dragon, looking like a Colossus on the back of his tiny Indian nag, rode up and joined them.

'Longhair's dead,' he said. 'They got him in the back. He didn't know what had happened. I couldn't do nothin' ... I had to leave him.' The last phrase rumbled out from between clenched teeth. In his queer half-primitive way the giant had been very fond of the little long-haired half-breed. The thought of even leaving his body back there among the devils he had fought so long was evidently repugnant to Dragon.

The other white men bowed their heads silently. Another fine man lost in this savage unsung war. There was nothing that could be said.

But suddenly Cody burst out. 'The train! Those devils an' the train. Death Ordey won't be able to stop 'em now even if he wants to. What the hell are we amblin' along for? We've got to ride!'

Events were reaching a climax in Julesburg too. The agitators and would-be street-lawyers were at their mischievous work again and the railroad workers were in a turmoil. They milled in the cart-rutted main drag and it was a significant fact that although they cried aloud for their belated pay, many of them seemed to have found enough money from somewhere to fill themselves with whiskey – or maybe somebody else had been filling them with it.

Among the tipsiest and most troublesome faction loomed big Mick, the Irishman. Mick was a good worker, a good fighter, a reasonable fellow, and a pard of Dragon, the buffalo-hunter. But strong liquor does funny thing to a man and the mighty son of Erin was no exception to the rule. Dragon was not there to drink with, to quarrel with him, to josh him out of the sullenness and stupor. All the carping workers needed was a leader, an imposing leader behind whom they could hide, a noisy fearless being who would breath fire and slaughter. Mick was it! – and his simple mind was uplifted and inflamed at their choosing him. All the worst elements of the half-savage crusading spirit of his ancestors rose to the fore in him. He would show these money-grabbing stingy spalpeens! His mates would have justice, by God, or he, Michael O'Halloran, would know the reason why!

Around him were gathered all the hard-cases of Julesburg and the U.P. as he marched from the biggest saloon. The crowd swelled alarmingly as they marched down the street. Luck was with them. They greeted their good fortune with a howl of triumph as Ralph Burndon and Judge Mackey came out of the frame-building in which the latter had his office. The two men stopped on the veranda, petrified for a moment by the blood-curdling sound. Then Judge Mackey moved back a little into the shadows. The younger man, however, stood his ground, his hands clenched on the veranda rail, his blond hair gleaming in the light that came from a nearby window.

The babble died down a little. A shrill voice yelled: 'We've played around long enough. Let's lynch the dogs!'

A few others took up the cry like simple children. 'Lynch 'em! Lynch 'em!'

But big Mike wanted no part of that. Even in his drink-fuddled mind he admired Burndon's courage as he stood there erect on the veranda.

'Hold your horses,' he boomed. 'We'll give 'em a chance to say something for themselves first. If we don't like what they say we'll tar an' feather 'em an' run 'em out of town. Maybe they'll find their way back to their bosses and get some of that money they owe us . . . Now then, Mr High-an'-Mighty Burndon, how about our money?'

Money was the cry now! The crowd took it up frenziedly.

'Quiet!' boomed Mick. 'Let the gintleman speak!'

There was ribald laughter and cat-calls, then comparative silence.

Burndon said clearly: 'You know as well as I do that General Casement has made a trip back East especially to look after your interests. He should be back soon. You've been very patient. If you'll just hang on a little longer I'm sure . . .'

His voice was drowned in a storm of ironical cheering and clapping. At this stage of the game flattery was lost upon them. 'What's the matter with the ol' Judge,' shouted somebody. 'Is he scared?'

'Yeh, what's the matter, Judge?'

'Come on out an' show yourself, you of bag o' bones.'

'What've you got to say for yourself, Judge?'

With startling suddenness the old man came out into the light. His hands gripped the veranda rail and he leaned forward across it almost as if he would leap down upon them. The crowd went quiet and his words dropped like vicious stones in the midst of them.

His voice rang, tremulous with passion: 'You scum!' he said.

There was more laughter but it had an ominous ring. Folks at the back began to jostle. The front ranks moved forward a little. But they were still waiting for a cue from the big leader who stood with rather a dazed expression on his broad, homely Irish face.

A horseman dismounted at the back of the crowd and hitched his mount to a rail. Then he began to worm his way through the press until he was standing close by the corner of the veranda. It was the man who called himself Jake Limes.

Burndon saw him. He started a little and jerked his head. The man bowed ironically. Leaning nonchalantly against the wooden pillar he produced a cheroot and lit up. With a gesture of annoyance Burndon turned away.

The other man seemed to come to a sudden decision. He had only taken a couple of draws from his weed but he tossed it, almost savagely away from him. Then he stepped on to the veranda and walked purposefully to join the other two. His tall, well built body had an easy grace. His first appearance was commanding. No great actor taking his first cue for the evening and striding on to the boards could have made a more dramatic appearance.

Julesburg was no out-of-the-way layout like the Pete Crow Ranch. As soon as the tall man stepped into the light he was recognized by people in the crowd.

'Bill Hickok,' said somebody.

The name passed from lip to lip. It didn't sound so good. When 'Wild Bill' took a hand in things somebody generally got hurt. Many of them had never seen him before, but they had heard his description from other lips. To see the man in the flesh was no anti-climax. He had the face and figure of a Greek god and the cold, unfathomable eyes of a man-killer. It was easy to believe the tales that were told about him. The mere sound of that fabulous name struck awe and terror into the hearts of the less hardened members of the crowd . . .

The pregnant silence was broken by the clatter of hooves and the yelling of excited voices.

The crowd scattered in all directions to make way for the horsemen who dismounted quickly at the steps. Major Frank North, Bill Cody, Bucko Martin and Dragon joined the others on the veranda.

There certainly was an imposing bunch up there now. It was fiery Major North who spoke, his voice ringing clearly and decisively.

'You want trouble do you? You want your money! Well, maybe you'd like to fight for it. The train that's bringing it to you is being attacked by Indians. I want as many men as I can get! Get your guns an' follow me!'

His pronouncement was like a bombshell dropped in the middle of them. They began to cheer and break away in all directions.

'What's the matter with yuh, Mick me boy?' boomed Dragon. 'Got cold feet?'

The big Irishman shook his boozy head and came to his senses. 'A foight is it?' he yelled. 'Oi'm your man!'

Fifteen minutes later a huge, motley force of horsemen with Frank North and his Pawnees at their head, streamed out of Julesburg and on to the plains. But Bucko, Cody and Dragon were not with them this time. They had other things to do. Hickok had vanished, but whether he was with the fighting force or whether he had gone off on some lone wolf campaign of his own nobody seemed to know.

Cody said: 'Ackroyd, La Brue, Kramer, Slim Jackson – they were with Ordey and the Injuns. All members of Bitter Creek's meat-party that were supposed to've been massacred. You saw 'em, Dragon.'

'Yeh, I saw 'em.'

'Can't you see it all now? It must be Bitter Creek an' his gang who're passin' rifles to the Injuns. They staged the massacre thinking to throw suspicion away from 'em for all time. Bitter Creek's leg-wound was faked. The vanished wagon was full o' rifles. The so-called dead men jest joined up with Death and his renegades. No wonder we could find no trace of anythin' or anybody when we went out there afterwards. What we got to find out now is where the rifles came from in the first place. Bitter Creek's our man. Come on.'

They were approaching the lodging house where Johnson hung out when they saw him coming down the street towards them. He saw them and turning, went into a small gambling-hell.

'That's the dive where most of his men gather,' said Cody. 'An' you can bet they ain't ridin' tonight. We'll have to watch our step. Easy does it.'

Side by side he and Bucko breasted the narrow batwings. Dragon towered behind and above them.

Business wasn't as brisk as usual, right now the whole of Julesburg was quieter and more deserted than it had ever been. But this little joint still had its clients.

Biter Creek was up against the bar. There was no one in his immediate vicinity but many of the players at the tables were members of his band.

His squinting eyes watched the three men as they came in. But his eyes gave nothing away.

Cody and Bucko were too cagey to barge directly across the room towards him and risk a shot in the back from one of his friends. They began to work their way in an interested manner around the tables where games were in progress. Dragon went in the other direction.

Neither of them ever got near their quarry. The dramatic entrance of the man who prevented them from doing so was characteristic of him. His boot thudded on the batwings as he kicked them open. He strode erect into the room for a few paces then paused and took a few more paces to the left so that his back was to the wall and there was nobody behind him. All the time he watched Bitter Creek.

He said: 'Hello, Red, I've been lookin' for you.'

The words were like a signal. On all sides men melted away from the tables. In a couple of seconds there was an empty space between the newcomer and Johnson.

If the latter had not recognized his man that morning in North Platte he knew him now.

Bitter Creek Johnson was not an unusually brave man, but he was a desperate man. He knew he had only one thing to do. Like many before him he hoped – and, although fear was like a lump of ice in his guts, he acted.

His hands were only on the butts of his guns when both of the other's weapons boomed deafeningly. With his back to the bar Johnson stood stiffly in a half-crouch, one hand on his gun, the other hanging lax at his side. His eyes glazed over and he swayed forward. Not until just before he hit the floor did his statuesque pose break and he disintegrated into something that looked like a shapeless bundle of rags.

Hickok's handsome face was drawn, his mouth stretched in a half-snarl. His cold blue eyes had a strange glow. He menaced the room with his two long-barreled guns. Only with a flicker of his eyelids did he acknowledge Cody and his two pards as, their guns out too, they ranged themselves each side of him.

'All right,' snarled Hickok. 'Clear the room. Everybody outside. Make yourselves scarce. If there's a man on the street when I come out of here I'll kill him quicker'n a rabbit.'

The four men moved away from the door, forming a tight circle with guns bristling in all directions as they backed into the centre of the room. Apprehensively, with nervous slowness the company began to leave. Nobody felt inclined to take any sort of a chance.

When the room was empty except for the four men and the crumpled thing on the floor, Cody said: 'I wish you didn't shoot so straight, Bill. We needed him to tell us where the Injuns are getting their rifles from.'

'Rifles!' echoed Wild Bill. 'Goddam it, so that's what they'd got in the wagons. I figured it was something pretty hot. No wonder they cut up rough when I wanted to take a look in 'em. I'd bin lookin' all over Julesburg for that copper-nobbed snake. I spotted him in the crowd before you came and then lost him again.'

'You talk in riddles, Bill,' said Cody. 'Why did you want him? An' what's this talk about wagons an' the rest?' Dragon came back from peering round the corner of the door. 'Not a thing in sight except a little yaller dawg,' he said with a leer.

Hickok told them about the early morning incident in North Platte.

He went on to say: 'I guess I know where they pick the stuff up. A ranch up along the Platte owned by a queer gink named Pete Crowe. He probably gets 'em himself by wagon along the riverside route. It's pretty safe an' quiet along there . . . I worked at the ranch for a coupla days cowpunching . . .'

He scowled as Cody grinned. 'Funny ain't it? That coupla days hard work's gonna cost the railroad plenty if I have my way.'

'I didn't know you were working for the railroad, Bill,' said Cody innocently.

Hickok swore. 'Neither did I till I got nosey. Anyway, I think I found where they store the stuff at the ranch. The straw-boss caught me snooping. He was an old acquaintance o' mine, gave me the slip when I was marshal an' after him for murder. Called himself Dick Boynton. Back in Abilene it useter to be Jim Cuthbertson. I recognized him from the first. His face is a give-away all the time, dead-white an' puffy, queer wishy-washy eyes. He didn't recognize me at first. I had to kill him . . .'

'Wait a minute,' said Bucko Martin. 'Had this queer-lookin' gink got his left arm bandaged-up?'

'Yes, now you come to speak of it, I remember he had. I noticed it the first time I met him up there.'

'Cody,' said Bucko. 'The stranger at Mother Brannigan's. The one Minnie slashed. It must've been him. He probably came here to contact the big man in Julesburg. I believe Death Ordey, Bitter Creek an' all the rest are jest pawns. There's a big man behind it all here. How else did Ordey get to know about the pay-train? Queer-face came here to contact the king-pin, the man we want.'

'Well, we didn't see much of him,' said Cody. 'But Ma Brannigan or Minnie might know more. If he had visitors or anything.'

'What are we waiting for then,' said Bucko and made for the batwings.

'Not that way,' said Hickok sharply. 'The back!'

The others trusted to the gunman's lightning reactions and followed him. He led them out of the back door and along an alley that led to the main drag. But he drew both his guns as he halted them at the corner.

He stepped around the corner and shouted, 'All right, friends.'

Two men started out of the shadows opposite the door of the gambling house. Hickok began shooting. One of the men did not have time to press the trigger before he was cut down. The other, somewhat of a sharpshooter, sent two slugs perilously close, one of them tipping Dragon's hat. Then this gunman too, crumpled up.

Another man broke from a point a little farther down the street and took to his heels. Dragon, cursing loudly, sped him on his way with a few shots at his heels. He disappeared in a doorway. The street was quiet and deserted once more. The two bodies were mere black shapes in the dusty shadows.

'Two more o' Bitter Creek's gunnies,' said Cody. 'The poor fools.'

Bill Hickok was chuckling softly.

TWELVE

When they reached the rooming-house its owner was standing in the doorway.

'What a sight for sore eyes you four are,' she said. 'Wuz you the cause of all the shootin'?'

'Kinda,' said Hickok.

'Come tuh the right place this time ain't yuh, Bill,' said the mountainous female with a horrible leer.

'Cut the cackle, you ol' hay-bag,' said Hickok. 'Let us come inside.'

Dragon, beside Hickok, gave Ma a shove with a rock-like shoulder. Cursing indignantly the old dame was spun out of their path. Even her fleshy bulk was not proof against the weight of the giant buffalo-hunter. As she turned to flounce away in mock unbrage Dragon pinched her bottom. With a screech she turned and swung at him. He dodged adroitly, he was used to such treatment from his squaw.

'Will you two big apes cut it out,' said Hickok. 'Sit down, Ma, we want to talk to you.'

The old lady's would-be coy simper made Bucko Martin shudder. 'Wal,' she said. 'If this is gonna be a party we'd better have some liquor.' Her voice soared suddenly, alarmingly. 'Minn-ie!'

'Yes, we want to see Minnie as well,' said Cody. 'And where's that kid Benny who hangs around here?'

'He'll be down at the Palladin havin' his supper, I guess. What is this: an inquest?'

Cody told her what it was, or at least as much of it as was necessary for her to know. Minnie arrived and Ma sent her for drinks.

The old lady did not prove to be of any help. She had only seen the queer-faced man Boynton twice, when she admitted him and when she turned him out. No, she didn't think he'd had any visitors while he was here. Leastways, not to her knowledge. Maybe Minnie would know more.

'At least she won't be so damn longwinded,' said Hickok maliciously.

The half-breed girl returned. The folks took their drinks. She turned away but Hickok beckoned her back.

'You'd better question her, ma,' he said. 'It's very important, but make it fast. An' take that scowl off your jib, it mars your natural beauty.'

'You big, smooth-faced sneering skunk.' said Ma. 'If I had a gun I'd shoot yuh dead.'

'Now, Ma,' chided Cody. 'You know he could beat you.'

'Yeh, that's all he's good fer.'

'All right,' said Hickok. 'I've let you have the last word. I hope you're satisfied. Now don't leave the girl just standin' there. Spiel!'

The deaf-and-dumb girl stood with feet twisted, head bent, very conscious of the hard stares of these four members of the sex she hated. But they were in too much of a sweat to be conscious of her rather blowsy charms. They only wanted one thing from her: knowledge – facts!

Ma clasped her arm to attract her attention. When need be she was quite gentle with her charge. The girl raised her head and fixed her big dark eyes on the old lady's hideous face with a look almost of worship in their depths.

Ma began mouthing and making complicated signs to her, asking about the man Boynton – Minnie had good cause to remember him – telling her he was a bad man, he sold guns to the Injuns. If Minnie hated men, she hated Injuns, of every sex and kind, even worse. She bobbed her head furiously with indignation, her hand instinctively moved to the knife in the band of her worn skirt.

'Get on with it,' said Hickok.

Ma glared at him and made more signs, coupled with the horrible grimaces of her hairy, meaty face. Minnie answered in kind, her eyes flashing now, her white teeth showing, her body twisting in rage. Then as Ma continued with her dumb play the girl's face became smooth, her eyes blank. She began to shake her head.

Mother Brannigan turned to the men. 'Can't get anythin' out of her,' she said. 'She says as far as she knows nobody visited that *hombre* while he was here.'

'Tell her tuh think,' said Hickok. 'Think! The man wasn't a hermit, was he? What did he do? Where did he go. . . ? Didn't she see him with anybody at all?'

The girl, her curiosity getting the better of her aversion, was watching the moving lips of the big handsome man.

Her brown face wore an almost agonized expression as she attempted to concentrate, she was utterly unused to mental gymnastics.

With facial contortions and gesticulations Mother Brannigan encouraged her.

Suddenly the half-breed girl's eyes glowed. But it was with diffidence that she communicated her thoughts to her mistress. Ma nodded understandingly, nodded another couple of times. Then she turned to the four men.

'The only person Minnie ever saw this *hombre* Boynton

with, was the old Jedge. She saw him go in the back way o' that place where the Jedge hangs out. Then she saw the two of 'em talkin' by the window.'

'Judge Mackey?' said Hickok.

'I can't believe the old Judge had anything to do with this set-up,' said Cody. 'Why, he's one o' the U.P's staunchest supporters.'

But Hickok's experience of lawmen had made him more suspicious.

'He's got just the front for it then. Respected citizen. Working hand-in-glove with the U.P. Who'd suspect him?'

'Aw,' said Cody. 'Probaby Boynton only called on him for some legal advice.'

'Probably. But it's funny that the Judge was the only person he was seen talking to. We figured Boynton came here to contact the king-pin didn't we?'

'Yeh, but naturally, their meeting would have to be in strict secret.'

'This meeting seemed to be secret. Boynton went in the back way . . .'

'We can't convict Judge Mackey on the evidence of this gel . . .'

'Nobody's convicting him!' said Hickok harshly. 'But he certainly needs investigatin'. I don't know the ol' goat like you do, but on the face of things I figure he want's watchin' – an' watchin' so's he don't know about it. If he is the king-pin he must be getting mighty leary right now.'

'The way I see it,' put in Bucko Martin stolidly, 'The Judge and Ralph Burndon are the main suspects because as far as we know they're the only people who are completely familiar with the U.P. plans.'

There was plenty of sense in that. Hickok turned to Mother Brannigan. 'Ask the gel about that smarmy galoot, Burndon,' he said.

The old dame did so. The girl shook her head vigorously. 'Burndon's never been near,' said Ma.

'The best thing we can do is go find Benny, that young clerk who helps out here,' said Cody. 'He might be able to tell us more.'

They discovered the pale, weedy youth having supper in the Palladin. His watery eyes looked alarmed as they approached. Then when he was sure that they meant to be friendly his eyes were suffused with hero-worship. What a fabulous killer like Wild Bill Hickok wanted with him he did not dream. He trembled a little.

It was Cody who spoke. 'We want you to answer some questions, Benny. If you give 'em plenty o' thought an' answer 'em as best you can you may be helping us a whole heap.' The four men grouped themselves round the table. The rest of the diners cast them covert glances of curiosity. They were ignored. There was nobody there it mattered about. Everybody who meant anything, except the late Bitter Creek's men, who were doubtless skulking in their holes, were out on the big raid.

Cody asked the questions, while Hickok interjected impatient remarks from time to time. The kid tried hard but he could not help them. As far as he knew Mr Boynton had not had any friends or visitors at all. He had made no more impression on Julesburg than if he had never been there before. Benny was an intelligent youth. He was also a very curious one. He watched the men's faces. When they mentioned Judge Mackey he almost wagged his prominent ears.

At length Bill Hickok said: 'Wal, we've got one lead – an' that'll have to be followed. The Judge'll have to be watched secretly.'

He looked round at the other three. Nobody spoke. They wanted action. The gunman looked at Benny.

'If I can be of any help, Mr Hickok,' said the youth eagerly.

Hickok looked at Cody, who shrugged, at the grim-faced Bucko, at Dragon. Then he leaned towards Benny.

'All right, son. You can help. But what you've got to do has got to be secret. It's government work an' if you breath a word of it to a soul I'll cut your liver out an' feed it to the buzzards.'

Benny recoiled a little. 'I wouldn't – I wouldn't dream of it, Mr Hickok.'

'An' no questions,' echoed the youth.

Hickok leaned nearer, lowered his voice and told Benny what he had to do. It did not take him long but when he had finished, Cody said:

'But he can't watch all the place at once.'

'No, you're right he can't,' said Hickok. He scowled. Then he turned to the youth again. It was any port in a storm now. 'Have you got somebody who'll help yuh? Somebody you can trust.'

The youth shook his head slowly.

'Goddam it!' said Hickok.

Benny's face puckered with anxiety. Then suddenly it brightened a little.

'Minnie 'ud help me,' he said.

'Minnie?' echoed Wild Bill.

'That deaf an' dumb half-breed wench?' said Cody.

'Yeh,' said the youth. 'She'd do it if I asked her. You know she can look after herself. An' she couldn't talk about it could she?'

'No, she couldn't,' said Cody. 'But a gel . . .' To his chivalrous nature there was something a little repugnant about using a woman for their purpose.

But the others weren't so scrupulous. To them the ends justified the means.

'Why not?' said Bucko Martin.

'If the kid say so I guess she'd do,' said Hickok.

'I don't know how he'll do it,' said Dragon jocularly.

'Minnie won't as a rule do anythin' for a man.'

'She'll do it if I ask her,' said Benny . . . 'Maybe she don't think I'm a man yet.' He added with unconscious irony.

'All right,' said Hickok. 'You get Minnie, pronto. You know what to do?'

'Yes, sir.' Benny rose from his chair with alacrity. His carriage had a new jauntiness as he left the eating-house.

'We've wasted enough time here,' said Bucko Martin, suddenly roughly.

He wanted to get his fingers round Death Ordey's scrawny neck, or get that skull-like face before the sight of his gun. All this time while they gabbed and theorized it seemed to him that his enemy was slipping away from him.

Dragon backed him up. It grieved the big fellow terribly to be missing any part of a fight.

'Right,' said Hickok. 'Let's ride.'

His words were almost drowned by a terrific peal of thunder.

'Here it comes at last,' said Dragon as he swaggered to the door. 'It's bin bi'ling up all night.'

'Wal, I guess I could do with a bath to wash some o' the Injun stink outa me,' said Bucko Martin.

As they rode out of Julesburg the rain was slashing at them viciously as if furious at being held in check so long. The elements bawled and thundered in triumph. The riders took their soaking stolidly and were refreshened by it and ready for the fray. The rain pelted with a steady rhythm and the dull skies began to lighten.

The plains of the Platte were bathed in silver and like a golden path down the centre of them ran the steel ribbons of the Union Pacific giving no hint in their shining splendour of the blood, sweat and tragedy that had gone into their laying and of the battle that was being fought over them at that very instant. The stars, clustering ever thickly, bathed them with an innocent light, but in the heart of at least one of the riders who followed their course they spelt only death and frustration . . . Maybe they would spell vengeance too before the night was out.

Suddenly above the rush and thunder of the rain they heard the shrill blast of a train whistle, cutting through the bluster of the elements like the piercing shriek of a banshee. As one man they checked their horses' galloping strides. The gleaming eyes of the Iron Horse approached along the rails. Cody rode his horse into the middle of the track, and oblivious of the rain that streamed down his face, took off his hat and waved it wildly above his head. The other three joined him.

'I hope they don't think we're hold-up men,' said Bucko.

But the monster drew up with a screech of brakes and already a familiar figure was leaning out on the foot-plate. Cody rode his horse forward, raising his arm in a half-salute.

'General Casement, it's certainly good to see you.'

The lean soldier greeted them all by their names.

'You got through all right then?' said Hickok.

'Yes, we came through. The storm was raging back along the line hours ago. It held us up. Frank North an' his army were already at grips with the redskins when we got to the point of ambush. They'd already almost wiped out a bunch of renegades they caught heaving logs across the line.'

'Death Ordey's bunch?' saisd Cody.

'No, another lot. Ordey came along with the redskins a little later.'

'Pete Crow's hands I'll wager,' said Hickok.

'We've got some of 'em under guard at the back o' the train,' said the General.

'How about the rest?'

'When the troopers from the train joined in the battle the redskins turned and ran for it. But it was the renegades we wanted. They made a break for it. When we came away most of the Julesburg faction were chasing them up towards North Platte. I suppose they figure to hole up there.'

'We'll ride on,' said Cody. 'We may be able to help.'

'All right,' said the General. 'I guess if we meet up with any more trouble my troops can handle it. But I don't think we shall. Those Indians certainly had the feathers scared off them. I guess the white men had promised them easy pickings. They had a disagreeable surprise.' He turned his head. 'All right, engineer, let's get on to Julesburg.'

The Iron Horse snorted and gushed steam. The mounts of the four men snorted too and pranced in alarm.

'Let's go,' said Cody.

They waved their arms at General John Casement and, as the train started off once more, set off at a gallop.

The rain was still pelting steadily, but now they hardly noticed it. Action lay ahead and, for one of them at least – vengeance!

They saw the glow of the fire long before they reached North Platte.

'Looks like they're smokin' 'em out,' said Dragon.

'Roastin' alive is too good for 'em,' said Hickok.

As they got nearer they saw the flames and heard the shooting. Then the shooting died down and finally, ceased altogether. The flames died down too as if North Platte, reborn for a few hectic moments, was sinking once more into oblivion.

As the four men rode down the trail which led to the old line-town other riders came out to meet them.

They were U.P. workers. One of them shouted: 'It's all over but the shouting.' His voice was a little tremulous and he was pale about the gills.

The four men rode on. In the town they passed a bunch of North's Pawnees with still-dripping scalps hanging from their belts. Then they saw Major Frank North himself come through the doorway of a rickety-frame building, the only one left standing in a small area of smouldering ruins.

He saw the new arrivals and greeted them. Behind him came his adjutant Captain Brian Plumb. Then, herded by the Corporal the Indians called Big Firestick and a bunch of Julesburg men, came a sorry and sodden-looking crew of Death Ordey's renegades. Bucko Martin's eyes gleamed as he looked for their leader.

North said: 'Did you get your man, Cody?'

'Yes. Or at least Bill Hickok did.'

The two notorious fighting men measured each other. The professional gunman and lawman who made his own rules, and the well-disciplined old soldier. Then the latter said:

'Glad to have you with us, Hickok.'

'I'm charmed, Major,' said the other with a mocking bow.

North turned towards the prisoners. 'Good job my Pawnees didn't get here first,' he said. He raised his voice: 'All right, Captain. Get 'em strung together.'

Firestick ran forward. 'Death Ordey's slipped away somewhere, Major. We can't find hide nor hair of him.'

North's lips tightened but he did not say anything. It was Hickok who spoke.

'I guess I know where Death's makin' for. We'll get him.' He wheeled his horse. 'See yuh, Major.'

Bucko Martin was right beside him as he rode down the street. Cody and Dragon were not far behind.

As they swept beneath the archway of the entrance to the Pete Crow Ranch the buildings before them seemed deserted, washed in the rain-haze. But as they got nearer a man scuttled across the yard.

'Stop,' yelled Hickok.

The man paused, saw himself menaced by four ominous-looking riders and stood in his tracks as through petrified.

'It's the cook,' said Hickok. 'He's purty harmless. I don't think he rightly knows what's bin goin' on here.'

The fat little man had recovered his poise a little as they reached him. He faced them boldly.

'What do you want?' Then recognizing the big handsome horseman. 'Oh, it's you, Limes.'

'Hickok's the name,' said the big man harshly. 'Where yuh bound for, Cookie?'

The famous name had come as a shock to the fat man. He looked a little deflated.

'I wuz goin' to tell the boss we'd got visitors,' he said.

'You were, were you? I ought to fill you full o' lead. But you fed me well when I was here so I'll spare you – in exchange for a little information.'

'Thanks,' said the cook with a show of bravado.

'An' if you lie tuh me I'll still fill you full of lead.'

'I ain't aimin' tuh commit suicide,' said the cook.

'All right. Who else is here?'

'Only the boss an' a couple of his pet gunnies. An' two more men who jest came. They're in the ranch-house. Go quietly around the back.'

'Thanks, pardner,' said Hickok. 'Now go back to your cook-house an' shut yourself in. No matter what you hear don't show yourself or you're liable to get your haid blown off.'

The cook nodded and scuttled away. The men left their horses and proceeded on foot. As they turned the corner of some outbuildings and moved down the alley with the ranch-house on the right of them the wind blew the rain like needles into their faces. Sweeping across from the plains and the Platte River it blustered and howled.

'It certainly is blowing up some tonight,' said Dragon.

The wind took his words and derisively tossed them away.

Cody said: 'One good thing, I guess they never heard us comin'.'

'We've got to take Pete Crow alive,' said Hickok. 'An' make him tell us who the king-pin is, to settle things once an' for all.'

They were unhurried, their urgency tempered with caution. All of them were too seasoned as fighters to risk spoiling things now their goal was almost reached. They wore their slickers over their gun-belts, careful not to let any moisture reach the death-dealing weapons snug in their sheaths.

The storm had taken on a new excess of violence, reaching its climax in a tirade of sound and fury. Although it would be almost impossible for the people inside the building to hear their approach, with the caution which had become ingrained in them through years of dangerous living, they went cat-footed, half crouching, their whole bodies tense and poised.

Bucko was in the forefront with Wild Bill. The young cowboy's nerves were stretched like fiddle-strings. His hand caressed the butt of the gun beneath his slicker. From time to time he shook his head so that the rainwater that had gathered in the crown and the brim of his Stetson cascaded to the ground before him. The storm was enough to put up with, nothing should be allowed to impair his efficiency now.

They seemed an eternity traversing that dark alley-way while Bucko Martin thought of his dead brother Lafe and of Tubby and Red . . .

What were the thoughts of the tall, handsome man beside him? This man who had seen so many fights, who lived with Death perched and leering on his shoulder, and carried it on each hip. A man's life was nothing to Bill Hickok. Did his own mean much to him? He had more than his share of health and physical looks despite the life he led. He was intelligent and he had an ice-cold brain and a muscular co-ordination that amounted to genius. He was an artist of action. Most of his sort died young. When was he to die?

THIRTEEN

They reached the corner of the ranch-house. Hickok who was nearest, turned it first. His breath left his mouth in a little hiss. His hand dipped. He had trouble with his slicker. It was the first time he had failed on the draw in such circumstances. It nearly cost him his life.

The slug chipped the cloth at his shoulder as the other man's gun boomed. Then both Hickok and Bucko were retaliating and the guard bounced down the veranda steps. All four men ran on to the veranda and fanned out, their guns ready now. Hickok, moving like a well-oiled robot, broke a window with his gun-barrel and sprayed the room beyond with a stream of hot lead. Even as he finished firing Bucko kicked the back-door open and charged through, followed by Cody and Dragon.

Judging by the outside architecture the ranch-house was a big ramshackle place. Somewhere in there were the men they sought. They did not hesitate.

A faint light shone under a door right opposite them. Bucko flattened himself against the wall beside it. Wild Bill came through the window. The faint light disappeared.

Bucko reached forward and lifted the latch of the door. He swung it open. It was Dragon who stood before it and fired two shots into the blackness. Then Bucko went through, throwing himself forward. A gun boomed to the right of him. Slugs fanned his hair. He lay flat on his stomach, gun elevated, and fired at the flashes. He heard a choking cry.

He heard a movement behind him, back brushing a wall, and knew one of the others had joined him. All was silent now at the other end of the passage.

There were more movements behind him then Cody's voice hissed 'We're all here.'

'We can't split up in this darkness,' said Hickok. 'Or we might be shooting at each other. Where did that shot come from, Bucko?'

'Down. Follow me.'

Bucko rose and ran lightly on his toes. They could just distinguish his dim figure. They followed. He bent over the still form on the floor.

'Seems like he's dead,' he whispered. 'But I cain't tell who it is.'

He fumbled, and cursed as his hand dabbled in blood. He wiped it on his chaps.

'He ain't long or thin enough for Ordey,' he said.

'Probably the second of Pete's gunnies,' said Hickok. 'Now we've got to find Crow, Ordey, and the man Ordey brought with him. An' if I don't miss my guess they're round this corner somewhere.'

'Yeh, I thought I heard somethin',' said Dragon in a husky whisper.

Hickok lay down on his belly and, shoving his gun around the corner, elevated it a little and thumbed the hammer. With a movement of his wrist he sprayed the passage with bullets.

Acrid gunsmoke filled the air and, even after the shooting had stopped, the echoes died hard and the detonation made the men's ears ring. As if in derision the rain seemed to thunder on the roof with redoubled violence.

Dragon gave an impatient snarl and turning the corner

began to lumber down the passage. A light showed dimly at the other end then, as the giant buffalo-hunter advanced, went out. Dragon hissed 'Look out,' and, with surprising swiftness, dropped his great bulk to the floor.

Somebody was fanning the hammer of a Colt. The slugs screamed along the passage. Cody gave a little hiss of surprised pain.

'Bill!' said Bucko.

'It's all right. Jest a crease.'

Dragon threw himself forward, rolling. Lying flat against the wall he opened up. Bucko joined him. Cody and Hickok slithered along, too. Their dim bulks stopped, crouching. against the opposite wall. The reverberations of Dragon's barking gun died away. Above the rush and patter of the rain came the thump of running feet.

'Come on,' said Bucko and springing to his feet almost flung himself along the passage.

He reached the door at the end and, taking a chance, grasped the handle.

'It's bolted or somethin',' he gasped.

The door groaned as he threw his weight against it.

'Outa the way,' growled Dragon.

Bucko stepped aside. The giant buffalo-hunter stepped back a few paces then, like one of the huge beasts that earned him his livelihood, charged. His massive shoulders hit the door squarely. It crashed inwards. Dragon sprawled. Already Hickok was covering him with shots. But there was nobody in the darkness beyond.

'You all right, big boy?' hissed Cody.

'Yeh. Come on.'

Another line of light glittered on the floor to the right of them. Bucko ran across the room, flung himself against the wall beside the door. Nothing happened.

Bucko wrenched at the door and cursed. He kicked it. 'Come on Dragon,' he said.

Hickok was reloading. 'I'll cover you,' he said.

Dragon lurched forward, his weight giving him impetus. This time he went right through, sprawling into the lamp-lit room. Hickok elevated his guns. But he did not fire. The room was empty.

Cody ran across to the window. 'Look out!' he shouted and ducked.

Slugs shattered the glass, ripped the curtain to shreds. Plaster and wood-chips flew from the opposite wall and a little line of holes appeared there. By that time the three men were lying flat. Cody was pressed against the wall beside the window. He looked out and saw the running man. Quickly, before he was out of range. He drew a bead and fired.

The man lurched forward as if he had been tripped. He fell on his stomach and lay kicking.

Bill Hickok ran out on to the outer porch. As he did so the wounded man rose, seemed to whirl in an excess of pain and rage, firing even as he moved. But his shots were wild. Both Cody and Hickok retaliated, with devastating effect. With a shrill scream the man went over backwards. This time he lay still.

Another man was running, with an ungainly limping gait, across the yard.

'Crow,' yelled Hickok. 'We want you. Better stop or I'll shoot.' He began to run after the ranch-owner.

The other three came out of the porch. 'Watch out, Bill,' said Cody. 'There's another one of 'em somewhere.'

They left the porch, fanning out. There was no sign of Death Ordey. Was it possible that he lay dead back there in the gloom of the house?

'Crow,' yelled Hickok. 'Stop, damn you, or I'll plug yuh.' But the ranch-owner continued to lope along like a crazy man. Hickok fired from the hip, from in the cover of his slicker. Crow sprawled forward on his face, got up on his knees, hopped forward a little like a strange wounded bird then flopped again and layed still.

Bucko joined Wild Bill. The latter said: 'He ain't dead. I jest hit him where he showed the most.'

They ran to the fallen man. He was still conscious. Hickok turned him over. His eyes looked up at them crazily. He gibbered with fear.

Hickok went down on his haunches in the mud. He lowered the muzzle of his gun to within an inch of the man's face. 'If you'll answer a couple of questions I'll promise not to press the trigger,' he said. 'Who's your boss in Julesburg?'

Crow's head wobbled with pain and eagerness. His eyes pleaded piteously as he tried to form words with his trembling lips. Then he got two out, strangled but clear enough, forming a name.

'Judge Mackey.'

'There,' said Hickok triumphantly.

'Where's Death Ordey?' said Bucko hoarsely. His dark eyes menaced the wounded man.

Now the words came out in a rush. 'He wants money. He's gone to Julesburg after the Judge . . .'

When the other two men joined Hickok, Bucko was already in the saddle. He set his horse at a gallop, hanging low over the saddle as the rain beat at him.

Jamboree in Julesburg. The train was in, the payroll was safe. And the conquering heroes were returning. They marched down the main drag with their prisoners and their wounded and their dead. The latter number were fortunately few. They marched and swaggered and yelled, teamsters, buffalo-hunters and workers rubbing shoulders with half-naked Pawnees with scalps in their belts and with troopers of the U.S. Army with carbines over their shoulders.

At his post in the shadow of a porch Benny heard the jubilant sounds and felt drawn towards them. He thought of the grim-faced, handsome Hickok and the job he was doing for that great man; and for that other great man, Will Cody, and the mountainous Dragon and that hard-looking cowboy from the Pecos. He stuck to his post. He seemed to have been standing there for years just inside shelter while the teeming rain formed a puddle before his feet. He fingered the big Colt in his jacket pocket. Mother Branigan had given it to him. He meant to use it if he had the chance. He was a man now not a scared kid.

He hadn't seen hide nor hair of the crotchety old Judge. He wondered how Minnie was faring at the back of the building. She was to fetch him if she saw anything.

He had been putting two and two together while he was standing here. He was no mug. He was pretty certain now what the old Judge had been up to. Personally he had always thought there was something false about the old goat.

Returning warriors were streaming past him now. They did not notice his slim figure in the shadows. One or two of them began to fire their guns into the air.

Fingers plucked at Benny's sleeve. It was Minnie. She pulled him, making motions for him to follow her. He did so. They ran around to Minnie's post in an old disused outhouse. She made motions towards the back of the building, then raised her right hand high above her head. Benny gathered that a very tall man had entered there. He left her and crept forward to investigate. He found the man's horse standing in a patch of shadow around the corner of the veranda. He returned to the girl. She leaned against him as they crouched and waited.

Out on the main drag the hullabaloo was dying down a little and here at the back among the outhouses and the ashcans there was quiet and the wind soughed from across the plains.

Benny clenched his fist around the butt of his gun as two men came out on the back veranda. One of them was the bent form of Judge Mackey. And even in the darkness Benny had no difficulty in recognizing the other as Death Ordey. The two men moved along the veranda and were lost in the shadows. Fearful of losing them altogether Benny said 'Stay here' to Minnie and ran out of cover. He vaulted on to the veranda and cursed as he realized the girl was following him.

He saw the two men again. They were standing still at the other end, the white blobs of their faces turned towards him. He realized he had been too hasty. They had spotted him.

A gun glinted in the thin man's hand. Benny screamed to the girl and threw himself flat. The gun boomed twice. Benny felt the wind of the slugs. He was sickened as he heard them thud into flesh behind him. Minnie fell across his legs, then rolled off. He did not need to look. He knew she was dead.

Something inside him snapped. Blood seemed to gush to his temples, filling his eyes with a red haze. He went beserk.

'You swine!' he screamed, tugging at his gun. He felt it in his hand. He rose to his feet, lurching forward, the gun held in front of him. It bucked in his hand as he pressed the trigger.

He felt a sharp blow in his right knee. His leg went from under him. Cursing frenziedly, tears of rage and pain streaming down his cheeks he tried vainly to rise.

His vision cleared a little and he saw Death Ordey leap over the rail and in to his horse's saddle. The old Judge ran away around the corner.

Ordey's horse broke away from the shadows, its rider bent low over its neck. Benny gritted his teeth and fired. The beast came to a dead stop as the slug ploughed into its side. It shuddered, then lurched suddenly to its knees. Ordey was thrown clear but temporarily stunned by the fall.

The sobbing Benny started to crawl towards him. Feet thudded along the veranda. Strong hands reached under Benny's armpits and lifted him to his feet.

The youth looked into the face of Bucko Martin the ex-cowboy.

'Minnie,' he choked. 'He got Minnie.'

'All right, son,' said Bucko gently. 'He won't get away with it now. You've done a good job. Rest easy.'

He propped the youth in a sitting position against the door-jamb. 'Stay there. I'll be back.'

Death Ordey was rising to his feet as Bucko went down the veranda steps. The bandit saw him, raised his gun and fired. He missed.

Bucko did not pause in his stride, but his hand dipped, he fired from the hip. Ordey saved his life by flinging himself desperately sideways. Then he darted for cover. Bucko fired again. The slug hit Ordey in the shoulder. He teetered and fell. He rose to his knees, cursing, frenziedly fanning the hammer of his gun.

Bucko's leg went from under him as a bullet seared his hip. He rose again and limped on. He thumbed the hammer three times and, through the blue smoke haze and the night, saw Ordey go down again, and lie writhing. With his last bullet Bucko made sure. Ordey lay still in the mud.

People were running out the back there now. A bunch of workmen gathered around Benny and the still form of the dead Minnie. Benny was not too badly wounded to tell his story straight, to hasten his revenge on the second of the men who had caused the death of the girl.

Judge Mackey a traitor! Hobnobbing with the renegade Ordey! The pack took up the cry. Judge Mackey! Many of them remembered how earlier that night he had called them scum. 'Get him!' they thundered. 'Get him!' And the hue and cry was on.

Bucko Martin swayed on his feet. He was soaked and bedraggled and his boot was beginning to fill with blood from the flesh-wound in his thigh. Also his gun was almost useless, dripping with rainwater. But he had to find the Judge.

He limped around the corner of the frame building. At the side was a small door. Bucko paused. Maybe the Judge had gone through there and was hiding somewhere in the building. The crowd wouldn't think of looking for him there. Bucko tried to put himself in the Judge's place. He was a clever and cunning old man . . .

The ex-cowboy made his decision. He limped to the door and tried it. It opened. Was that good? He almost turned back. But his hunch was too strong for him, he had to follow it through.

He stepped silently into the darkness. He closed the door softly behind him. Now the blackness was impenetrable. He stood awhile until things began to take shape around him. He was in a kitchen.

He distinguished the dark oblong of another door. He crossed to it and opened it gently. It squeaked a little. He held his breath as he slid through the aperture. The room he found himself in was lighter. There was a window and through it Bucko saw the moving heads of the mob. Their clamour rose in his ears. He wondered if, somewhere in this building, an old man crouched and listened to it too. Bucko felt no pity for him.

He opened another door and moved into a hallway. Up ahead were the stairs. On tiptoe Bucko began to climb them. But his wounded thigh made him awkward. He stumbled. He cursed inwardly and stopped climbing. He thought he heard a sound from up above. He kept perfectly still. He could hear his heart thumping and his breathing seemed unnaturally loud. He smiled grimly to himself. All he seemed to be doing tonight was creep around in dark houses.

The storm had been on for hours. Now it was beginning to lose its bluster but the rain still fell steadily as if it never intended to stop.

Bucko gripped the stair rail and, wincing as his wound made itself felt, hauled himself forward. He climbed steadily again and reached the landing. He stood tensely. Some mysterious sense told him he was not alone. He flattened himself against a wall. 'Judge Mackey,' he called.

There was no answer but he heard movements behind the door nearest to him.

'Judge Mackey,' he said again, more softly this time. He reached out a foot and scraped the door. He drew it back just in time, as a gun boomed and bullets slashed through the panels.

Bucko showed his teeth. He was tired of this cat-and-mouse business. He let his body fall, hitting the floor with a rumbling bump. He lay still by the door.

He heard the old man moving about inside. He reached a long arm up for the latch, lifted it. The door gave. He flung it inwards and dived in on his hands and knees. His hands caught hold of a pair of skinny legs through the cloth of trousers. Then something hit him with stunning force on the back of his head.

He was aware of the old man jumping over him. When he sat up the Judge was running down the stairs. He tumbled down the last few steps.

'Stop, you ol' fool,' yelled Bucko.

He heard the running footsteps going along the passage. He rose and gave chase.

The Judge was making for the side door. He reached it and ran through right into the arms of a bunch of workmen who were seeking him.

Bucko heard the roar of triumph. When he reached the door they had already carried the kicking, screeching old man out into the main drag. Bucko leaned against the door, panting. His leg felt as if it was immersed in scalding water. He had a job to keep on his feet.

Presently he left the doorway and hobbled down the alley to the wide, cart-rutted street, ankle-deep in mud and water. The rain was slowly abating as if the elements at long last had confessed themselves beaten by human fury. Human fury that was unleashed in primeval savagery as a howling mob carried Judge Mackey down the main street of Julesburg.

They halted finally outside a big feed-barn. Someone flung a rope over the jutting beam. For a moment there was a strange awful silence. Then it was broken by a single drawn-out sound, a cross between a howl and a sigh.

After that the crowd began to melt away. Pretty soon there were very few people in that section of the street.

Bucko Martin limped along. He stopped and looked up at the dangling, sodden thing that had been his enemy. Three more men came along the street and stopped in the shadows behind him. Although he did not turn around he knew they were there. His gaze wandered from the wretched hanging carrion and on along the street, up the slope that led to the Julesburg cemetery. For a moment he saw the faces of the three who had died. He bade them silent farewell. Then he turned around to face the fabulous living.